TWO DOGS
IN A TRENCH COAT

Go to School

TWO DOGS
IN A TRENCH COAT

Go to School

by Julie Falatko
Illustrated by Colin Jack

Scholastic Press/New York

For Matt, who started it all

CHAPTER ONE

Waldo was pacing the perimeter. He was a small and scruffy dog who smelled like **kibble** plus something else he'd rather not discuss.

Waldo walked from room to room, checking all the doors and windows. What was he checking for? **Stray meatballs.** Squirrels. (Squirrels were a real threat, and required constant vigilance.) He also had to check for his humans. Every day they escaped, despite Waldo's best efforts. He begged. He pleaded. He made his eyes extra sad. And still, every day, they escaped. Somehow.

Even though the humans got out every day, Waldo was the best at his job. Had a squirrel ever gotten into the house, for instance? No. Never. And while he had yet to find a **stray meatball**, he was very good at finding odd bits of **cheese** around the refrigerator, and he cleaned them all up, as a good dog should. He was a professional.

Sassy was a lot bigger than Waldo. She had helped him pace the perimeter earlier, but then they got to the part of the front hall with the wood floors and her back feet kept slipping and then she was lying down and then she was napping.

Every afternoon a square of sun came in the window and made a warm spot on the floor. It was very important for Sassy to nap in the sun square every day. It was her job. She also kept the squirrels out of the house. (Had there ever been a squirrel in the house? Not a one.)

Sassy was the best at what she did. Not only did she keep all the squirrels away, but she also let the humans rub her belly, which they loved to do.

Sassy had reached the good part of her nap where the sun was so hot it was like a blanket of fire, plus she was so relaxed she couldn't move. The only thing ruining this stellar nap was Waldo. He kept walking by her head and clearing his throat, which sounded like a bullfrog doing a dog impersonation.

"How can you sleep when there are so many squirrels and imminent intruders?" asked Waldo.

Sassy lifted her head. She sneezed. The sun made her sneeze, and whenever she sneezed, she sneezed *fifteen times* in a row. "There are intruders?"

"Imminent intruders. That means there might maybe be some in the next year."

"That's not really what that means," said Sassy.

"Also our humans might be back at any second!"

"You know they won't be home for another twenty-two minutes. I'm going back to sleep."

"There's something else we need to talk about," said Waldo.

"Are you sure? Because I need to nap."

"Something absolutely must be done about this school situation."

"Oh, fine," said Sassy, sitting up. "Let's do something about it. But what?"

It had been going on for a while. Every day Waldo and Sassy's boy, Stewart, trudged off to this awful place called school. Waldo and Sassy knew it was awful because every night Stewart's parents asked him what he did at school, and he said, "Nothing." Plus he smelled like a weird mix of boredom and anxiety. This school place was clearly the worst.

"I've got a plan," said Waldo.

"Oh, really," said Sassy.

"What, you don't think it's a good plan?"

"You haven't told me what it is yet."

"You're always so negative, Sassy," said Waldo.

"I'm not being negative, you just haven't told me what your plan is."

Waldo padded around the room. He checked the doorways and looked under the table. He made sure there wasn't a spy near the refrigerator and got distracted by a **muffin crumb**.

Sassy yipped to get his attention. "Hey! Mr. Investigator! What's your plan?"

"Oh, right," said Waldo. "Like I said, we need a plan to deal with the school problem. So, are you ready?"

"Yes," said Sassy.

"Maybe you should sit down. It's a good plan."

"Fine." Sassy sat.

"Maybe you should lie down. Maybe we should both lie down for a bit."

"Just tell me the plan already!"

"The plan is . . . well, first, we get an airplane."

"Oh biscuits, are you kidding me?" said Sassy. "Where are we going to get an airplane?"

"I don't know. The airplane store? Or order it from that internet thing?"

"No. Shh," said Sassy. "Someone's coming!"

"What do you mean, 'shh'? Let's bark!"

The dogs commenced the standard Bark and Waggy Greet procedure, to remind the humans that the Waldo and Sassy Household Protection and Face-Licking Service was as relevant as ever.

Stewart sat on the floor to pet his dogs. He was a rumpled kid who didn't mind some dog slobber on his cheeks or muddy pawprints on his jeans.

"You're the best dogs in the world," said Stewart. "You're better than all the humans."

"He's just stating facts," said Waldo.

"Kid's speaking the truth," said Sassy, licking Stewart's chin.

"If he likes us that much, why doesn't he give us **hot dogs** all the time?" said Waldo.

"That's a good question," said Sassy.

Just then Stewart's dad walked in, and the dogs Waggy Greeted him, although he was more reserved than Stewart, and they'd learned they weren't allowed to jump on his pants to lick his elbows.

"Hey, kiddo," said his father. "How was school?"

Stewart sighed. "Boring." Sassy met Waldo's eye. Yep. This school problem was just as bad as ever.

"Well, great," said Stewart's father. "Good for you. You know what I always loved about school? Lunch. Oh boy, lunch was great. When was the last time I had a **bologna sandwich**? Why don't we eat those anymore?"

"Yes," said Sassy, "I have no idea what a **bologna sandwich** is, but my inner dog sense is telling me it would be fantastic."

"I didn't have a **bologna sandwich**," said Stewart. "I ate the lunch you packed for me this morning."

"Oh, right."

"This is worse than I thought," Waldo told Sassy.

"Why?"

"I saw that **sandwich** the father made. It had **sprouts** and **low-fat soy cheese**. The side dish was **tiny carrots**."

"I like **tiny carrots**!" said Sassy.

"Better than **bacon**?"

"No, of course not. You know what would be good?" said Sassy.

"**Bacon** wrapped around some of those **tiny carrots**," said Waldo. "But never mind that. What I'm saying is, Stewart must be seriously glum to have eaten that lunch."

"Our poor Stewart."

Waldo closed his eyes for a moment in deep concentration. "I think," he said, "that we have to make sure Stewart never leaves the house again."

CHAPTER TWO

Waldo and Sassy knew their plan was foolproof. They had been practicing it for years, really, what with their ongoing desire to have the humans hang around all the time.

"We're going to do a double slink front-and-back with supplemental hand licking and preventative shoelace untying," said Waldo.

"Got it," said Sassy. "And I'll be ready to block the door." Sassy always blocked the door. She was bigger. And hairier.

"Should we practice it again?" asked Waldo.

"No, we should probably rest," said Sassy. "Save our energy."

"Here they come! Get ready for invasive following!"

Stewart came down the stairs and put his backpack by the front door. Sassy moved it three feet to the left before joining Waldo and Stewart in the kitchen.

"I moved his backpack," whispered Sassy. "He'll never find it. He'll have to stay home."

"Good thinking! Get ready. I'm going in." Waldo slumped onto the floor and put his chin on Stewart's shoe. He whined. He moved in closer. "Stewart's eating a **fried egg sandwich**," said Sassy.

"I know that," said Waldo. "You think I don't know that? I've never smelled anything more **fried egg sandwichy** in my life."

"He's enjoying it," said Sassy. "I think he'll probably savor it all day. That's what I'd do if I were a human. I'd eat **fried egg sandwiches** all day long. And share them with my dogs. Why isn't he sharing that **fried egg sandwich**? He should!" Sassy barked once at Stewart, who ignored her.

"You're getting distracted," said Waldo. "Hey, he's done!"

"What, already?"

"He's getting up! Evasive maneuvering! Evasive maneuvering! This is not a drill! Shoelaces! Backpack! Crying! Sad eyes! **Hamburger!** Block the door!"

"What do you mean, '**hamburger**'?"

"What?"

"You said '**hamburger**.'"

"I didn't. Why would I say '**hamburger**'? Unless you think Stewart's got a **hamburger**?"

"I don't think so?" said Sassy. "I only smelled the **fried egg**."

"They should eat **hamburgers** for breakfast."

"They should eat **hamburgers** for every meal! Why don't they do that?"

"I'm hungry."

"Me too. Oh! Listen! Breakfast!"

The dogs ran to the kitchen to the sound of **kibble** filling bowls.

Two minutes later, the dogs looked up and realized the house was quiet. Too quiet.

"They escaped again!" said Sassy.

"How?" said Waldo. "How do they do that *every day*? We were blocking the door."

Sassy raised a furry eyebrow at Waldo. "Not while we were eating, we weren't."

"Oh. Right."

"They got us with their Breakfast of Distraction."

"What do we DO?" asked Waldo. "Every day— EVERY DAY—they escape, and Stewart goes to that horrible place where he does nothing all day, and the parents go somewhere that leaves them smelling like printer ink and sticky notes and very bad coffee. I don't understand. Why would they leave? Why would they choose to leave this house and go to those awful places?"

"Could be we're missing some facts."

"No, I'm sure that's not it," said Waldo. "I think they're being hypnotized. They're under a spell."

"That doesn't make any sense."

"Sure it does! Don't you see? We have to save them from the evil overlord who is controlling their brains."

"Don't forget about the work we have to do here too. We can't just leave."

"Can't we though?" said Waldo. "Why not?"

"Who would protect the house? What if there are squirrels? Or those . . . what did you call them? 'Imminent intruders'?"

"We can get up early," said Waldo. "We can protect the house for the hour before breakfast, and then save our humans from the evil overlord. We'll be back by dinner."

"Okay," said Sassy, walking slowly around the room, checking windows, and thinking. "Let's say we do that. Let's say we can save Stewart, at least. How? How do we get out there?"

"I really think my airplane plan is a good one," said Waldo.

"No."

"A drone might work."

"No."

"Police car?"

"No."

"**Hot dog** cart?"

"Oh, maybe! Wait, no."

"We could just follow Stewart to school."

"What?"

"Just follow him. Wait until he leaves and go after him."

"You know what? That's actually a good plan."

"Now can I have an airplane?"

"No."

CHAPTER THREE

Except following a kid to school, if you're a dog, isn't so easy.

They got out the doggy door easily enough, but then they were stuck in the backyard. First they got rid of all the squirrels in the yard. (It didn't take long, since there weren't any to begin with, which just proved what excellent and professional dogs they were.) They spent five minutes trying to jump over the fence, and another ten minutes of Waldo lecturing Sassy about "this is why my airplane plan would have been better."

They dragged all the patio furniture together to make a ramp, hoping to "run like a gazelle" (Waldo's words) and "leap like a lion" (Waldo again) until "we soar majestically like beautiful eagles to the other side of the fence" (yep, Waldo). Instead they "ran like hedgehogs until we crashed into the chairs and got our paws caught in the seats while they fell on our heads" (that's Sassy).

Then they napped for a bit.

Finally Sassy realized she was big enough to stand up, put her paw on the latch, and open the gate.

"Well, you would have saved us a lot of time if you'd done that two hours ago," said Waldo.

"Never mind that now," said Sassy. "Let's find Stewart."

Stewart had gone to school hours ago, of course, but his scent was easy enough to track, and in a few minutes they were at the front door of a big brick building with a sign out front that said BEA ARTHUR MEMORIAL ELEMENTARY SCHOOL AND LEARNING COMMONS.

"What do you think this place is?" asked Waldo. "Some kind of factory?"

"It looks like a **sausage** marketing corporation or a **ground beef** prison or maybe a **meat** testing plant," said Sassy.

"Those are oddly specific options."

"Something smells **meaty**, is all. Come on, let's look in the windows."

Waldo hopped onto a bench near one window and peeked in. "Children. At tables. Using crayons."

"That sounds horrible!" Sassy looked into another window. "This one is a bunch of books. Good **gravy**, there are books everywhere! And children are pulling books off the bookshelves and looking at them!"

"That is shocking and awful. What about that one?"

"There are children in there!" said Sassy.

"And?"

"They are watching some kind of giant television. It appears to be dancing pencils?"

"What torture!"

"Waldo?"

"Yes?"

"I'm not entirely convinced that any of this is awful. I'm seeing lots of pillows, frankly. And fuzzy rugs. That room with all the books had a whole raised platform covered in carpet, and the sun was shining in on it. Everything in there looks cozy. Plus there's that persistent **meat** smell."

"So it's either a horrifying torture factory, or a nice place to take comfy naps?" said Waldo.

"One of those, yes."

"I guess we'll have to go inside and see for ourselves."

But the entryway to the school presented a new set of problems.

The doors had handles. Sassy jumped up and pawed at them, but they were locked.

"Maybe we should just wait until the end of the day," said Sassy. "Or go home and nap? I'm pretty tired."

"Focus, Sassy! We came all this way!" said Waldo. "We can't give up now!"

Just then a lady in a cardigan sweater walked up and pressed a button on the wall next to the door.

"HELLO," blared a voice from the wall.

"Hi, Dottie, it's Lindsay," said the woman in the cardigan. Then the door buzzed, and she opened it and went in.

The dogs looked at each other. "This is too easy," said Waldo. "Let's go!"

Sassy stood up and pressed the button on the wall.

"HELLO," said the voice.

"Arf!" said Sassy.

"HELLO?" said the voice.

"Hiiiiiii, Doodie," said Waldo.

"What on earth just happened?" asked Sassy.

"Just get ready to open the door."

But the door never buzzed. Instead a short lady opened the door and stuck her head out.

"What are you dogs doing here? Who was here with you?" she said. "Shoo! Go on now! Go home!"

The dogs just stared at her.

Another lady, this one tall and stern, showed up behind the short lady.

"What's going on, Dottie?" said the tall lady.

"Someone tried to get buzzed in, but they sounded . . . well, they sounded like a robot. Or a child. So I came out here and all I found was these two dogs."

"We don't have time for dogs," said the tall lady. "Dogs! Leave!"

Before they knew what they were doing, Waldo and Sassy were halfway home.

"Ugh, I don't like it when alpha humans boss me around," said Sassy. "I'm not strong enough to disobey." She sat on the sidewalk.

"You're not even strong enough to make it all the way home," said Waldo. "Look at you. Come on! Get up! We've got work to do! I have a new plan."

"First you need to tell me when you learned to talk like a person."

"That's all part of the plan," said Waldo.

CHAPTER FOUR

Seriously," said Sassy, as they crawled back through the doggy door into the house. "Since when can you talk grown-up? The only human who can ever understand us is Stewart, but I think that's more of a mind reading thing. I thought you could only talk Dog."

"I can talk Human," said Waldo. "I learned it from a video."

"Okay," said Sassy. "So you can sound like a human. This is great. This is news. Though now that I think on it, I'm not sure what we can do with it. Should we get a phone and make a series of calls to our state representative?"

"No," said Waldo. "That's ridiculous. What we're going to do is go to the school, and get in."

"We already tried that. They don't let dogs in."

"Then we have to pretend to be something other than dogs."

"This is all so tiring!" said Sassy. "Can't we nap?"

"No time for that. We need a disguise."

After realizing the only things they could disguise themselves with in the kitchen were a lampshade and the garbage can, the dogs explored the parents' closet.

"Here! This is just the thing!" said Waldo, slipping on a long blond wig. He looked in the mirror. "I look like a surfer. This is great. I'm wearing this all the time from now on."

"I don't know why the parents have that, but you still look like a dog to me," said Sassy. "Oh, how about this?" She pulled a flowery dress over her head.

"You look okay," said Waldo, regarding her. "I guess.

Oh, look what I found!" He pulled a brown fuzzy pelt out of the closet. "What is it?"

"I don't know," said Sassy. "Put it on and find out."

"It's huge," said Waldo. "What is this thing?" He wriggled halfway in.

"Is that . . . a horse costume?"

"Apparently. Can you fit in the back end?"

"A. I don't want to be the back end of a horse. And B. What good is it going to be for us to try to get into the school as a horse that can talk Human?"

"It's really cozy in here, Sassy. Come on in."

"Now you need to focus. What else is there?"

Waldo took off the inexplica-ble horse costume and nosed back into the closet. "Hey, this might work!" He turned around to show off a big fake mustache.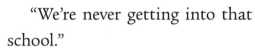

"We're never getting into that school."

"Wait, I found something!" said Waldo. "A detective coat!"

"I want to be a detective," said Sassy. "Pull it out."

"I can't reach it. You stand on my shoulders and grab it."

Sassy stood on Waldo. Waldo made a noise like a lawn mower that had run over a rock. Sassy got off Waldo.

"You squashed me!" said Waldo.

"What did you think was going to happen? Maybe you should get on my shoulders."

Waldo hopped onto Sassy's shoulders. "I'm so tall up here! I can see everything!"

"Can you reach the coat now?" said Sassy.

"Yes!" Waldo pulled the big tan trench coat off the hanger, and it fell over both of them. "Hey, look at us! We're a human! La la la, look at me, human talking, just a regular old human, that's me."

"We do look like a human," said Sassy. "A hairy human, but still."

"This will totally work!" said Waldo. "I'll stand on you, we'll wear this trench coat, and we can totally pretend to be a human."

"And then what?"

"I have no idea!" said Waldo. "Maybe we'll be tall enough to climb in through a window?"

"I'm not going to be tall enough to do anything if I don't nap first."

"Fine, fine, I have some important squirrel work to do anyway. First thing tomorrow, we do this trench coat thing."

"After breakfast, right?"

"Are you kidding me? This might be the most important thing we ever do! Of course after breakfast. No way I'm doing this on an empty stomach."

"It's a deal."

CHAPTER FIVE

$\mathbb{A}$nd so, the next morning, Waldo and Sassy woke early. They checked the perimeter for squirrels (all clear). They checked the kitchen for abandoned **cheeseburgers** (all clear, unfortunately). They ate their breakfast, and they put on their disguise.

"I'm still not sure we can do this," said Sassy as they practiced walking in front of the mirror. "This doesn't look right. We look like a poorly designed human who is about to fall apart into dogs."

They fell over, rolling apart and out of the trench coat.

"Don't be so negative, Sassy. We can do this. I'm going to need you to be strong. I wasn't going to bring this up earlier, but I found a secret stash of **dog treats**. Maybe we should raid it now. To keep our strength up."

"Yes please," said Sassy.

Waldo stuck his snout under the parents' dresser and pulled out half a bag of **liver treats**.

"Holy **biscuits**, how long have you been keeping that a secret?" asked Sassy.

"Twelve seconds," said Waldo. "I saw it right now when we fell down."

Buoyed by the remnants of fairly old **liver treats**, the dogs practiced for a very intense two minutes, until they managed to walk, Waldo balancing on Sassy's shoulders, without falling over.

"I really like this coat," said Waldo. "I look boffo."

"Speaking of boffo," said Sassy, "how exactly are we going to pull this off?"

"What do you mean, 'speaking of boffo'?"

"Huh?"

"What?"

"What?"

"You said 'speaking of boffo,'" said Waldo.

"It's, you know, just a way to change the subject. I have no idea what 'boffo' means. It sounds like a kind of **sausage**."

"I think it means 'awesome,' but maybe you're right. It's **sausage**."

"Fine."

"Good."

"SO. Speaking of **sausage**," said Sassy, "is the plan to casually walk in and then find Stewart and save him? Are we going to pretend to be a school inspector? A **meat** salesman? A ninja? Oh yes! Let's be a ninja!"

"Ninjas don't wear trench coats."

"They might."

"Nope," said Waldo. "We're wasting time. Let's go down there and do this. We need to save Stewart and come back in time for our three o'clock squirrel surveillance."

The dogs went out the doggy door and ran to the school. Sassy held the trench coat in her mouth, and Waldo scampered beside her. It was faster that way. When they got to Stewart's school, they hid behind a bush and put the trench coat on.

"Still no plan, then?" said Sassy.

"Look, we're going to walk into the school, and then, my dear Sassy, just leave it all up to me. I'll take care of everything. I'm a master improviser. Just you wait. You're going to be so amazed. It's going to be amazing."

"Is this how you plan on convincing them? Because I'm not convinced."

"I'm going to say whatever I think of at the time. It'll take too long to come up with a script. Come on. Let's go."

"You're going to say whatever you think of?"

"Yep."

"What are you thinking of right now?"

"**Pepperoni!** I mean, pulling off this plan. Code name: **Pepperoni**."

"Yeah, this'll be great. I predict we'll be kicked out within four minutes."

"Don't be so negative! Let's do this."

Waldo could reach the button by the front door, now that he was standing on Sassy's shoulders.

"HELLO," said the speaker.

"I am a new stooooodent," said Waldo.

"Just a minute," said the speaker.

Dottie opened the door and stuck her head out. "Hi there! New student, huh? Where are your parents?"

"The parents drink bad coffee in an office," said Waldo.

"Well, for gosh sakes, just get in here, then," said Dottie. "We'll get you signed right up!"

CHAPTER SIX

M s. Barkenfoff," Dottie yelled into the principal's office as she held the door open for Waldo and Sassy. "Good news! We have a new student!"

"Well, hello there," said Ms. Barkenfoff.

"It's the scary alpha human from yesterday," Sassy whispered up to Waldo. "I want to nap now."

"Keep standing!" said Waldo.

"What's that?" asked Dottie.

"Nothing! It's good! I am standing!"

"Alrighty, then. I just need you to fill out this form, and we'll find a spot for you in a class."

"I cannot."

"I'm sorry?" said Dottie.

"I cannot fill out a form. That is why I need school."

"Well. Sure. Okay," said Dottie. "Why don't you tell me your name?"

"Uh," said Waldo. "Sass-Wald-uh . . . Salty!"

"Salty?"

"Yes! I'm Salty!"

"What's your last name, Salty?"

"Woof! Uh. Dog. Ing. Ton," said Waldo.

"Oh **kibbles and bits**, this is a disaster," whispered Sassy.

"Okay," said Dottie. "Salty Woofadogington." She held up the paper she was filling in. "Did I spell it right?"

Waldo looked at the paper carefully. "Yes."

"Are you new in town?"

Waldo put his nose in the air. Something smelled good. "Yes."

"Where did you move from, honey?"

"**Liver**," said Waldo. Something smelled like **liver**. Then he realized that he'd just said "**liver**" in response to where he'd moved from, and he said, "**Ohhhhhhh**."

"Liver, Ohio?" said Ms. Barkenfoff. "I went to college near there."

"**Yes**," said Waldo.

"Now, the first thing we do with every new student," said Dottie, "is give them their own Bea Arthur Memorial Elementary School and Learning Commons T-shirt. It's our little way of saying 'welcome' and giving you some Bea Arthur pride and school spirit!" Dottie walked over to a shelf stacked high with neatly folded T-shirts.

"If we have to wear a T-shirt, they'll see the bottom half of you is a dog," whispered Sassy. "Also the top half."

"**No**," said Waldo.

"What's that, honey?" said Dottie.

"**No thank you to the T-shirt**."

"Everyone gets a T-shirt. It's okay!"

"**No thank you**."

"Maybe if they have a really huge one that covers both of us?" whispered Sassy.

"Do you have one in my size?" Waldo asked Dottie. "I am size XXXXXXXXXXXL."

Dottie stood back a moment and looked at Salty. "Well, I . . ."

"Also I am cold," said Waldo. "I like to wear my coat at all times. It is a special coat. I must wear it always and at all times. That is what we do in Liver, Ohio."

"Well, okay. I'll just give you the biggest T-shirt I can find, and you can keep your trench coat on."

A new lady came into the office, moving with swift efficiency. "What's that? Someone doesn't want a T-shirt? Who wouldn't want to wear a T-shirt declaring their allegiance to our fine school?"

Waldo and Sassy tensed. This was Stewart's teacher. They could smell it. Or she was a grown-up who spent a lot of time in Stewart's classroom.

"This lady is our **meatball** for getting closer to Stewart," whispered Waldo.

"She's a **meatball**? She smells human."

"No, that's a detective term. A **meatball** is the one who helps bring you closer to the victim."

"A. I don't think that's true," whispered Sassy, "and B. I'm hungry."

"Ms. Twohey!" said Dottie to the lady. "This is a new student, Salty Woofadogington."

"I'm from Liver, Ohio," said Waldo.

"Well, well," said Ms. Twohey. "Really. Liver, Ohio. And yet you still refuse a Bea Arthur Memorial Elementary School and Learning Commons T-shirt to show your school spirit."

"Uh. Correct," said Waldo.

"We have plenty of T-shirts," said Ms. Twohey. "Everyone gets one."

"I'm not the kind of human who wears a T-shirt," said Waldo.

"I see," said Ms. Twohey. "Are you the kind of human who would try to steal a teacher's lesson plans?"

"I do not think so," said Waldo. "I am from Liver, Ohio."

"Liver, Ohio," repeated Ms. Twohey.

"Yes," said Waldo.

Ms. Barkenfoff emerged from her office. "Oh, Ms. Twohey, you've already met Salty. Wonderful. Looks like you've got space in your class. Salty, this is Ms. Twohey, your new teacher. She is a wonderful teacher."

"Yes," said Waldo. "Correct."

Ms. Twohey squinted at Waldo. "It *is* correct. I *am* a wonderful teacher."

"Correct," said Waldo. "Yes. I am in your class now."

"Yes you are," said Ms. Twohey.

"We should walk there," said Waldo. "I am a new student now."

"Indeed," said Ms. Twohey. "Right this way."

46

Waldo and Sassy walked behind Ms. Twohey down the hall. "She suspects something," whispered Sassy.

"No kidding," whispered Waldo. "We have to be extra careful."

"Did you say something?" said Ms. Twohey.

"In Liver, Ohio," said Waldo, "we whisper to ourselves when we walk down school hallways."

"Really?"

"Yes."

"Well, here we are. My classroom. Salty, I want you to know that I take learning very seriously. We are all here to learn as much as we can. I don't tolerate any mucking about."

"I will not be barking about."

"Well, good," said Ms. Twohey. "Are you ready, Salty? Ready to enter the most enriching and educational room in this whole school?"

"I am ready," said Waldo. "I am from Liver, Ohio."

"Yes you are," said Ms. Twohey. "Let's go." And she put her hand on the doorknob and opened the door.

47

CHAPTER SEVEN

Wow," said Waldo as he and Sassy walked into Ms. Twohey's classroom. "This is the most enrichable and educatory classroom I've ever seen."

"We've never seen any classroom," whispered Sassy.

There were posters. Mobiles hung from the ceiling. A skeleton stood in the corner.

"I would like to sit near the skeleton, please," said Waldo. "In case I get hungry."

"In case what?" asked Ms. Twohey.

"I'm from Liver, Ohio," said Waldo.

"What are you doing here?" Stewart came over to his dogs. He recognized them immediately.

"Oh, hello," said Waldo. "We are here to save you from the evil overlord."

"Do you know Salty?" asked Ms. Twohey.

"Who?" said Stewart.

"Yes," said Waldo. "We are uncles."

"Uncles?" asked Ms. Twohey.

"Uncle aunts. Cousin friends. Fraternal nincompoops. Second **hamburgers** once removed."

Sassy nipped Waldo's foot to get him to stop talking.

"Our parents are friends," said Stewart.

"Yes!" said Waldo. "That sounds good."

"Well, that's nice. Salty, you can sit next to Stewart. I'm sure he'll help you get settled. But first come to the front of the room so I can introduce you. Class, this is a new student, Salty. Please make Salty feel welcome and get up to speed on all of our academics, since I'm

sure Salty's other school wasn't as wonderful and rigorous as our classroom. Salty, why don't you tell us a little bit about yourself?"

"I am Salty," said Waldo.

"Anything else?" said Ms. Twohey. "Do you have some favorite things you'd like to tell us about?"

"Yes," said Waldo.

"What are they?"

"Yes," said Waldo. "I like **hamburgers**. That skeleton is nice. Stewart is my uncle. I'm from Liver, Ohio."

"Well, we'd better move on," said Ms. Twohey. "Take your seat." Waldo and Sassy walked over to the desk next to Stewart and casually moved the chair to the side so Sassy could lie down.

"Now, students," said Ms. Twohey. "As you know, your big project is due in one week. I know you have all been working hard on your projects and will be ready to present your absolute best work. I  will remind you that you all must include a properly filled out Information Sheet with your presentation. The Information Sheet is what I will base ninety percent of your grade on. The Information Sheet is crucial. Do not neglect your Information Sheet. Without a properly-filled-out Information Sheet, you have no hope. You will fail."

"Stewart is sweating," Sassy whispered to Waldo.

"I know. He smells nervous," said Waldo.

"Hey, Salty, what's up?" said a boy behind the dogs. "What kind of a name is Salty? Is your sister's name Peppery?"

"Ignore him," said Stewart softly.

"Hello, human boy child," said Waldo, turning to face the boy. "You smell like frozen meat products that were not heated through properly."

"Whatever, Salt-man. I'm Bax. Bax the bully."

"**That is very straightforward**," said Waldo.

"That's just who I am."

"**Fair enough**," said Waldo. He turned to Stewart. "What is this big project?"

"It's a presentation we have to do. We have to pick a topic and study it for months and then present our findings in front of the class."

"That sounds neat," said Waldo.

"I guess," said Stewart.

"How is it going?"

"How is what going?"

"The big project," said Waldo. "The Information Sheet."

"Okay. It's fine. Don't worry about it. It's cool. I have it under control. It's all fine."

"That Information Sheet sounds like fun," said Waldo.

"Really?" said Stewart.

"What is that delightful smell?" whispered Sassy from under the trench coat.

"Not Bax, you mean?" said Stewart. "Smelling like **uncooked meat**?"

"No, something else," said Waldo. "I can smell it too. I've been smelling it all morning. **Liver and sausage**. Maybe **hamburger**. It just . . . it smells like a giant pile of **meat**. Where is that coming from?"

"I think that's lunch?" said Stewart.

"SIGN ME UP FOR LUNCH!" said Waldo.

"Salty?" said Ms. Twohey. "Everything okay?"

"**I am hungry**." Waldo made his eyes big and sad.

"Stewart, why don't you and Salty go down a little early so you can get settled in the cafeteria."

"**That is a great plan, Ms. Twooooarooohey!**" said Waldo, mistakenly howling a bit in excitement. "**You really are a good teacher.**"

"Oh, Salty, thank you."

CHAPTER EIGHT

I still don't understand what you're doing here," said Stewart as they walked down the hall.

"We are your dogs," said Waldo.

"You are our boy," said Sassy.

"But most dogs don't pretend to be a person and sign up for school," said Stewart.

"That is because they are not geniuses," said Waldo.

"Like we are," said Sassy.

"You can't save your boy when you're in the back-yard patrolling for squirrels," said Waldo.

"Save me from what?" asked Stewart.

"School," said Waldo. "But first let's talk about cafeteria. What is cafeteria? Is it where the **meat** factory is?"

"I guess?" said Stewart. "No, wait, there's no factory. The cafeteria is where we have lunch. Here it is."

"This place?" said Waldo, looking at the tables lined up in the huge room.

"Yes."

"I can smell delicious lunch but also sweaty sneakers and trumpet spit valves. Human school lunch is different from human home lunch."

"We also have gym here. And band practice."

"So we just eat lunch food?" said Waldo.

"I'm not sure you could call what they serve for lunch 'food.' Oh, gross, it's **sloppy joes** again."

"I have never smelled anything more delicious," said Waldo.

"I don't think they even use new **meat**. I think they recycle all the **meat** from previous weeks."

"That sounds wise," said Sassy.

"It won't seem so wise after you taste it," said Stewart. "Here, grab a tray, get in line."

"This is fun," said Waldo.

"Tell her what you want to eat," said Stewart, pointing to the woman standing behind the food.

"I will have all the **sloppy joe**, please," Waldo told her. The woman took a plate with a **hamburger bun** on it and scooped **shiny brown meat** on top.

"Is that good, or you want more, hon?" she asked.

"I **want more**," said Waldo. "**As much as I am legally allowed to have**."

She scooped more **sloppy joe** onto Waldo's plate and put it on his tray. Waldo picked up the tray, leaned over, and ate all the **meat**. And the **bun**.

"No!" said Stewart. "You're supposed to sit down at a table first."

"Why?" asked Waldo.

"Didn't I just give you food?" the lunch lady asked Waldo, looking at his clean plate.

"I do not think so," said Waldo. "I do not remember any food."

"You want **egg salad** or **sloppy joe**?"

"**Sloppy joe**, please," said Waldo. "A lot of it."

"Save some for me," whispered Sassy.

"I will try," whispered Waldo.

"You'll try what?" asked the lunch lady.

"I will try to eat all your **sloppy joe meat** so you don't have to save it for next week."

"You're funny, kid," said the lady.

"I'm from Liver, Ohio," said Waldo.

"Don't eat it yet," said Stewart as Waldo put his nose near the **meat** on his plate. "Sit first."

Sassy sat. Waldo almost dropped the tray.

"I mean come over here and sit at a table," said Stewart.

Sassy stood and they made their way to a table.

"Can we sit with you?" said Waldo.

"Of course! You're the best dogs in the whole world. It's nice having you here."

"We will save you," said Waldo.

"Hey, quit gabbing and start passing some of that **meat** down here," said Sassy.

Waldo dumped half the **sloppy joe meat** from the plate onto the tray. He regarded the lunch for a minute, then pushed a bit more of the **meat** onto his tray. Then he gave Sassy the plate. She ate the lunch in twelve seconds.

"Was that half?" asked Sassy. "I'm still hungry."

"Oh yes," said Waldo. "That was half."

"But you got to eat the whole first plate by yourself. You should have given me all the **meat** from this plate."

"That does not make any sense," said Waldo. "Don't worry, though, I'll go back for thirds."

"You don't get thirds," said Stewart. "You're not even technically supposed to get seconds."

"What?" said Waldo. "That's ridiculous!"

"I'm going to faint from hunger," moaned Sassy. "I need to nap immediately." She lay down abruptly, causing Waldo to fall halfway and almost out of the trench coat.

"Do you want the **tiny carrots** from my lunch?" Stewart asked.

"Yes, please," said Sassy, perking back up. "Are they wrapped in **bacon**?"

"No," said Stewart.

"I will eat them anyway," said Sassy. "Thank you."

"School is fun," said Waldo. "Every day you say it is boring, but it is not. There is **meat** and a skeleton of bones. There is a bully who made a joke that was not very good. I got two piles of **meat**. There are big projects and free T-shirts. Also **meat**. And I've heard a rumor about sneakers to chew on."

"Hey, look who it is," said Bax as he put his tray on the table. "I'm going to eat my **sloppy joe** with you today."

"Sometimes Bax sits here," Stewart said.

"Hello, Bax the bully," said Waldo. "Are you enjoying your **meat**?"

"No," said Bax.

"I liked it," said Waldo. "I will finish yours if you do not want it."

"It wasn't too SALTY for you?"

"Your jokes are terrible," said Waldo.

"Hey, Stew and Salty," said Bax. "You should get some friends named **Carrots** and **Beef** and **Potatoes**, and then you'd have a whole meal."

"Are you hungry all the time like I am?" asked Waldo. "Is that why you always talk about food?"

"I'll bet you're hungry all the time," said Bax.

"That is correct," said Waldo.

"I. Well, yeah," said Bax.

"I'm done with lunch," Stewart said to Waldo. "Are you done eating?"

"Will they give me any more food?"

"No."

"Then I am done eating."

"Let's go."

"Goodbye, Bax the bully. Have fun eating!"

"You have fun eating," said Bax, "your salty food."

"Yes!" said Waldo. "I have fun eating all my food. See you in the educational classroom!"

CHAPTER NINE

Back in the classroom, Salty drew a picture of a plant cell. He memorized his multiplication tables. He read a book about sharing. And he licked the skeleton's thigh bone.

Ms. Twohey talked more about the big project, and the importance of the Information Sheet. Waldo and Sassy listened intently. They liked rules. They liked being told what they were supposed to do. They knew how it worked: Humans said what the rules were, and if you followed the rules, you got a **cookie**. It was a good system.

"All right, students," Ms. Twohey was saying. "Thank you for all your hard work today. See you tomorrow."

Everyone stood and started putting their coats on.

"What is happening?" Waldo asked Stewart.

"School's over. It's time to go home."

"Already? I was not done. I am having too much fun. I do not want to go home."

"Sorry, guys. I guess you can come back tomorrow."

"Tomorrow?"

"Today is Wednesday. School is five days a week."

"Wednesday?"

"I'm sleepy," said Sassy, lying down suddenly, the trench coat pooling around her.

"Come on, guys," said Stewart. "Let's go home."

"I am confused about tomorrowday," said Waldo. "I am also sleepy. We will nap now. Good night."

"GUYS," said Stewart. "You can't nap now. It's time to go home! You can nap at home. Come ON."

"It's too late," said Waldo. "We're already asleep. We've never been so comfortable. I was sleepy and there was a carpet square and now I'm sleeping."

"Fine," said Stewart. "You can stay here. But I'm going. Also **meatballs**." Stewart walked out of the room.

"Good night," said Sassy.

"**Meatballs?**" said Waldo.

"What?" said Sassy. "Where's Stewart?"

"**Meatballs!**" said Waldo.

"Really? **Meatballs?** Where?" Both dogs were standing now. Waldo hopped on top of Sassy and they ran into the hallway, where Stewart was putting on his backpack and closing his locker.

"Hey, guys," he said. "Ready to go home?"

"I heard something about **meatballs**," said Waldo.

"Really?" said Stewart.

"Isn't it **Meatball** Wednesday?" said Sassy.

"That's not a thing," said Stewart.

"It is where we're from," said Waldo. "We're from Liver, Ohio."

"No you're not," said Stewart. "And you fall for that **meatball** trick every time."

They left school and started walking home.

"School is great," said Waldo. "You said it was boring, but it's not. There's **meat**. And books."

"You weren't there long enough to know how it is," said Stewart. "You didn't do any work."

"I did work! I am a working dog! Bax is nice."

"Bax isn't nice," said Stewart. "He told you himself that he's a bully."

"He doesn't smell like a bully though," said Waldo.

"Waldo's right," said Sassy. "He smells distinctly non-bully."

"What does a bully smell like?" asked Stewart.

"Angry sweat," said Waldo. "Glue. **Strange cheese**."

"Old dirt," said Sassy. "Unread books."

"Old dirt?" said Stewart. "Isn't all dirt old?"

"No," said Waldo.

"Gosh no," said Sassy. "New dirt is the best. Old dirt is sad."

"But Bax does not smell like any of those things," said Waldo. "He smells like a cocker spaniel."

"I don't always know what you guys are talking about," said Stewart.

"We don't always know what you're talking about either!" said Sassy. "That's fun."

"We're home!" said Waldo. "Finally. School takes a long time."

"You were barely there half the day," said Stewart. "And you didn't want to leave when it was time to go."

Stewart opened the latch to the backyard and the dogs immediately broke apart and out of the trench coat. They ran in long, looping figure eights in the grass for several minutes, and then came panting back to Stewart, who was watching them from the back steps.

"That felt good," said Waldo.

"I'll say," said Sassy. "Okay, everyone out of my way. There's a patch of sun inside that is calling my name. Nap time."

Waldo yawned. "Nap time. How do you stay awake all day at school, Stewart?"

"Sometimes it's hard," he said. "But you get used to it."

That night at dinner, the dogs watched Stewart.

"How was school, Stewart?" asked his mom.

"It was pretty good actually," said Stewart.

"Well, that's good to hear," said his dad. "What I wouldn't give for a **bologna sandwich**."

"I hope you're enjoying this **casserole**," said the mom.

"Oh, the **casserole** is great, great," said the dad. "What are they teaching you in school these days?"

"You know," said Stewart. "Stuff."

"Math? Are they teaching you math?"

"Yeah, Dad," said Stewart, laughing. "They're teaching us math."

"Did you hear that?" asked Waldo. "He said school was pretty good!"

"And he laughed at something," said Sassy. "That's a relief. We're done. We never have to go back to that place again. We can nap here all day."

"You know what I loved about school?" said the mom.

"**Bologna sandwiches?**" said the dad.

"Projects! Long projects that took months to prepare!" said the mom. "I really loved working hard."

"Oh, you," said the dad.

"Huh," said Stewart.

"We have to go back," Waldo told Sassy. "Look at him." Stewart looked at his lap. He closed his eyes.

"I know," said Sassy. "He is not loving this long project that is taking months to prepare. We have to help him."

CHAPTER TEN

Waldo and Sassy walked down the school hallway the next morning, dressed as Salty. "Hello, Doodie!" said Waldo. "Hello, human student! Hello, other human student! Good morning, Ms. Twohey! What a lovely day to be learning things!"

"Yes it is," said Ms. Twohey. "I see you're not wearing your school T-shirt."

"You are not wearing your T-shirt either," said Waldo. "We're twins!"

"I teach better in this pantsuit," said Ms. Twohey. "The children have to see me as an authority figure. I always wear this Bea Arthur lapel pin to show my school spirit."

"That is a nice pin," said Waldo. "You are a good teacher."

"Yes I am," said Ms. Twohey. "I know other teachers want my secrets. Or to take me down. They want to know my secrets and to take me down."

"Correct!" said Waldo.

"It is?" asked Ms. Twohey. "What do you know? Who are you? Did they send you from Don Knotts Technology and Arts Learning Academy two miles from here? Or are you on a mission from a secret group of teacher spies?"

"I'm from Liver, Ohio!"

"Uh-huh."

"Time for learning!" said Waldo.

The dogs walked into the classroom and took their seat next to Stewart.

That morning, Ms. Twohey read the class a story. The students worked on multiplication problems. They wrote essays about insects and had a snack. The dogs did not know they had to bring a snack, so Ms. Twohey gave them **pretzels**. They ate the **pretzels** and the bag the **pretzels** came in.

"School is so much more fun than you said it was," said Waldo.

"You're only on day two," said Stewart.

"Is it like this every day?"

"Pretty much."

"This is the most fun place," said Waldo.

"Except we can't nap," said Sassy.

"Time for gym!" said Ms. Twohey. "Line up here and change into your sneakers if you need to."

"Who is Jim?" asked Waldo.

"Gym class," said Stewart.

"Who is Jim Class? Is he a man who will give us **sausages**?"

"No, no, it's exercising. Running around. Playing sports."

"This day keeps getting better and better! Gym class sounds amazing."

The students walked in a line down to the gym (which was also the cafeteria). Waldo couldn't help smiling at the thought of it all. And drooling a little.

"**This room always smells incredible!**" said Waldo as he entered the gym.

"That's the attitude I like to see. You must be the new kid." The gym teacher was wearing a baseball cap that said RUN UNTIL YOU BARF and had four whistles around his neck.

"**I'm Salty**," said Waldo. "**I'm from Liver, Ohio.**"

"Welcome to gym," said the teacher. "You can call me Coach. Get ready for the cardiovascular experience of your life. You're going to work hard. You're going to play hard. You'll be part of a team, and you'll push yourself harder than you ever have before. You'll be screaming in pain and sweating buckets."

"**This sounds fun!**"

"I like you, kid."

"**I lick you too, Coach.**"

"You want to take that coat off?"

"**No, thank you.**"

"All right, kids, listen up," said Coach, blowing a whistle. "Today we'll be going outside for Ultimate Frisbee. It's like football, except we're not allowed to play football, so we play it without helmets and with flying discs instead. You all have to run your patooties off. I don't want to see anyone walking. Let's go!" He blew a few more whistles a few more times.

The class jogged halfheartedly to a field behind the school. Sassy almost started sneezing when a beam of sunlight hit her nose through the front of the trench coat, but she swallowed and managed to stay quiet.

Coach gave blue mesh pinnies to half the class, blowing his whistle repeatedly and for no apparent reason. He pulled a Frisbee out of a bag, blew his whistle three more times, and threw the Frisbee to the blue team. Waldo and Sassy had laser focus on that Frisbee. They forgot about **sloppy joe meat**, about squirrels, and about saving Stewart from any evil overlord. All they wanted was that Frisbee.

The game started in earnest, with one blue team member flinging the Frisbee to another. Just as it was about to be caught, Salty, racing as fast as Sassy could run, jumped into the air and caught it. Waldo chewed the plastic with satisfaction.

A kid on Salty's team yelled, "Salty! Here!"

"**What**?" said Waldo, and the Frisbee fell out of his mouth. One of his teammates caught it. Sassy ran down the field, and Waldo tried to yell but was so excited he just barked. No one seemed to notice. A kid from the other team got hold of the Frisbee, and she threw it high and wide. Everyone started running. Sassy got low and galloped, and then, at the perfect

moment, leapt high into the air, where Waldo again caught the Frisbee in his mouth, landing in the end zone. His team cheered.

"It's kind of weird that you catch it with your mouth," said Bax.

"It's not weird," said Waldo. "That's how we do it in Liver, Ohio. You should try it."

"This kid right here is showing the kind of vim and vigor I want to see from all of you," said Coach, blowing his whistle for emphasis. "Sprinting! Leaping! Diving! Why are you lying down now, kid? You should be pumped up and raring to go!"

"I am tired," said Waldo.

"Are you going to barf?" asked Bax.

"No thank you," said Waldo.

That night, the dogs could barely get off the rug to eat their dinner.

"The pooches sure are zonked out today," said Stewart's dad.

"I guess they got some exercise," said Stewart, smiling to himself.

"I got an email from Ms. Twohey today," said Stewart's mom.

"Oh?" said Stewart.

"She said you all have been learning multiplication and that in history you're going to start studying the American Revolution."

"Yep," said Stewart.

"She also said something about a big project."

"Oh yeah. Big project," said Stewart.

"I love big projects!" said Stewart's mom.

"Oh, you sure do," said Stewart's dad.

"You let me know if you want me to help," said Stewart's mom. "I bet you're already done."

"Okay," said Stewart. "Yeah. May I be excused?"

"Sure thing, buddy!" said Stewart's father.

"Our boy," said Waldo to Sassy, barely awake, "has a lot more to do on his project."

"I know," said Sassy. "I can smell it."

"Me too."

CHAPTER ELEVEN

The next day the cafeteria served something called All-American Mishmash. There was **meat**. There were **noodles**. There was **sauce**. There was **cheese**.

"There is **meat** again today!" said Waldo.

"I think it's more recycled **sloppy joe meat**," said Stewart. "But I actually like this one. There's a lot of **cheese**."

"That is fantastic news. This is such a great school."

Stewart and the dogs got their lunches and sat at a table by themselves. Coach came through the door of the kitchen, carrying a tray piled high with bowls of All-American Mishmash.

"Gotta feed the team!" said Coach.

Waldo and Sassy looked at the tray, drooling. They stared very, very hard at that blue plastic tray carrying so many bowls of delicious **meaty noodley goodness**. They used their dog brains to do a trick not many people know about.

Coach tripped over something invisible and dropped the entire tray of All-American Mishmash onto the floor right by Salty's feet. The dogs lurched forward, Sassy moving deftly under the trench coat so no one would see her, and swallowed the food in four gulps. The dogs slid back into their seat and Waldo casually pawed at his fork.

"What did you just do?" said Stewart. "Did you just eat all that food?"

"It is possible," said Waldo.

"We told him to drop it," said Sassy. "With our minds."

"What?" said Stewart.

"It is a thing we can do sometimes," said Waldo. "If we concentrate very, very hard we can make humans drop their **meat**."

"It doesn't always work," said Sassy.

"But when it does, it's great," said Waldo.

"Where'd it go?" said Coach. "I just fumbled a little, and lunch disappeared."

"You have to go get more, I guess," said Waldo.

"I guess I do," said Coach.

"Don't do that again though," said Stewart to the dogs. "At a certain point, they're going to notice that you're eating it all."

"Our job as dogs," said Sassy, "is to work right up until that point."

"Well, you're all done with lunch anyway, so let's go before Coach comes back."

The dogs reluctantly followed Stewart out of the cafeteria and walked back to class, where Ms. Twohey was waiting for them.

"I am so sorry that you didn't join our class in time to do the big project," Ms. Twohey said to the dogs. "I know you would just love it. Especially the part where you fill out the Information Sheet."

"That does sound like a lot of fun," said Waldo. "Does it?"

"Yes?"

"Or is that the sort of thing you'd say if you were a spy?"

"I am not a spy. I am from Liver, Ohio."

"Or is *that* the sort of thing you'd say if you were a spy?"

"It is not," said Waldo. "Can we do gym class again today?"

"No, Salty," said Ms. Twohey. "Today we have music."

"Do we run and catch in music?"

"You'll have to run to catch the melody because your singing is so bad," said Bax, coming up next to Salty. "You'll have to run out of the room entirely."

"I have misunderstood the word 'melody.' Is it like one of those balls with a squeaker inside?"

"You wish," said Bax.

"I do wish," said Waldo.

"Line up for music, everyone!" said Ms. Twohey. Salty lined up behind Stewart.

"I am excited for music," said Waldo. "There might be running and catching."

"Who told you that?" said Stewart. "There's no running or catching."

"Bax told me," said Waldo. "Bax is my friend."

The class walked down the hall and into a room with two pianos, a drum set, recorders, and tambourines. A lady sat at one of the pianos, and as the children walked in, she sang a song.

"Welcome children
Here's the thing
Ooka ooka ooka
It's time to sing!"

"Why did she say 'ooka ooka ooka'?" whispered Waldo.

"No one knows," said Stewart.

"What happens if we press this thing here?" asked Waldo as Sassy put her foot on a silver rectangle near the drums. A large mallet swung forward and hit the bass drum.

"Hey, that is a fun noise!" said Waldo. "Do it again!" Sassy pressed the pedal experimentally a few times, and then found her rhythm. It was like scratching her belly with her back leg. But more musical.

Waldo sang to the beat of Sassy's drumming.

"Hello, humans.
This is fun.
Ooka ooka ooka.
When do we run?
Hey there humans–"

"Okay, thank you so much," said the lady, jumping up from the piano. "Aren't you an enthusiastic one!"

"Yes, I am a good boy," said Waldo. "I am Salty. I am from Liver, Ohio." Sassy had to concentrate extra hard not to wag her tail.

"I'm Mrs. Gargle," said the lady. "Do you have experience in music?"

"No, not really," said Waldo. "I like to make noise and have everyone pay attention to me though."

"That's practically the same thing," said Mrs. Gargle. "Let's get started."

The students sat on the floor in a circle.

"Last week we worked some more on 'Oh Great Mountains and Wild Plains,'" said Mrs. Gargle. "Let's start again from the top."

The students all took deep breaths.

"Oh great mountains,
And wild plains,
Vast dense forests,
Where majesty reigns."

The children attempted some sort of harmony, but they sounded terrible. Waldo loved it. As the students took another deep breath to begin the second verse, Waldo took a deep breath too. It didn't matter that he didn't know any of the words. He could feel the music deep in his soul.

The children began singing again. *"So many buffalo . . ."*

Waldo pointed his nose toward the ceiling and howled a long, low howl. He ended up hitting more of the correct notes than any of the children did.

"Salty, that sounds wonderful!" said Mrs. Gargle. "Children, Salty is showing us a good example of how we sing better when we're properly warmed up and singing from deep in our bellies. Was there a particular warm-up you did today, Salty?"

"**Woof!**" said Waldo.

"That's a new one to me," said Mrs. Gargle. "Let's all try that together, children. Woof! Woof!"

Everyone started barking. Stewart rolled his eyes.

"This is the most fun I've ever had in music class," said Bax. "Good job."

"You are very good at barking," said Waldo. "You could be a dog."

"Hey! Watch your mouth!" said Bax. "Maybe *you* could be a dog."

"Maybe I could," said Waldo. Sassy nipped at Waldo's paw. "Ow! No, no, I could not. I could not be a dog. I am a human child from Liver, Ohio."

"Whatever," said Bax. "Woof! Woof!"

The children eventually stopped barking, and their next attempt at singing "Oh Great Mountains and Wild Plains" was, indeed, much better.

CHAPTER TWELVE

That night at dinner, Waldo kept humming to himself. He couldn't get the song out of his head.

"What does Waldo keep grumbling about?" asked Stewart's dad.

"Beats me," said Stewart.

"You know who was so grumbly today?" asked Stewart's mom. "Brenda. She ran out of sticky notes and I thought she was really going to lose it. Yep. You want to see a worked-up Brenda? Take away her sticky notes."

"Well, I sure know how that feels!" said Stewart's dad. "Can't get work done without sticky notes!"

"And tape!" said Stewart's mom. "Oh! Highlighters! I love those."

"Boy, office supplies are so great," said Stewart's dad. "We have so much fun. If you're lucky, son, when you grow up, you'll get to work in an office. Office supplies are almost as fun as school supplies. I sure am envious that you get to play with school supplies all day."

"That's not really what I do," said Stewart. "Do you play with office supplies all day?"

"Pretty much!" said Stewart's parents in unison.

"And do big projects!" said Stewart's mom. "We do a lot of big projects. That's another reason being a grown-up is so fun. Big projects all the time! Every big project you do now in school, is just preparing you for life as an office worker. You're so lucky!"

"What a time to be alive!" said Stewart's dad.

Waldo hummed some more.

"I think the dogs need to go out," said Stewart. "May I be excused to take them for a walk?"

"Sure thing!" said Stewart's parents.

It was a nice night. Waldo hummed while he and Stewart and Sassy walked down the sidewalk. Stewart was quiet, looking straight ahead, while the dogs smelled the trees and grass to see what the neighborhood dogs were up to.

"Bitzy got a new collar," said Sassy.

"Amos ate the **roast chicken** his people made for dinner," said Waldo.

"Waffles is a good girl," said Sassy.

"Sir Pepperton is in love," said Waldo.

"Squirrel!" said Sassy. The dogs perked up their ears and pointed their noses at the squirrel, who fluffed its tail tauntingly across the street. Sassy whined. Waldo hummed a song that was, in his opinion, extremely menacing.

"Come on, guys," said Stewart. "Leave it."

The dogs ignored him. They pulled on their leashes. There was a squirrel, and it was their job to defend their home. The squirrel continued fluffing. The dogs were on high alert.

"Ch ch ch ch ch," said the squirrel.

Waldo growled.

"Calm down, Waldo," said Stewart.

"After what he said?" said Waldo.

"What, the squirrel? What'd he say?" asked Stewart.

"He said 'nanny nanny boo boo' in Squirrel," said Sassy.

The squirrel looked at the dogs, pointed its little finger toward them, and leapt up a tree trunk.

"Now!" said Waldo, and they both bolted toward the squirrel. Or, that was the plan, but since they were attached to leashes, and this was nowhere near the first time they'd tried to chase a squirrel up a tree, Stewart was ready and had braced himself.

"Leave it," said Stewart again.

"I don't want to leave it," said Waldo.

"It is our job," said Sassy. "Our job might not involve sticky notes, but keeping that squirrel away is our job."

"It is our big project," said Waldo.

"Squirrels aren't a big project," said Stewart. "They are a little project. They are literally a tiny, fluffy, little project."

"Individually, sure," said Waldo. "But all of them together is big. You might not realize. Because we are so good at it. We keep so many squirrels out of the house."

"You do?" said Stewart.

"You bet," said Sassy. "We're professionals. And if all dogs did as good a job as we did, there would be no squirrels at all."

"They'd all go to Squirreltown," said Waldo.

"Squirreltown?" said Stewart.

"Squirreltown is where all the squirrels will go," said Waldo.

"One day, all the dogs will do such a good job that they will get rid of all the squirrels, and all those squirrels will live in Squirreltown," said Sassy.

"And, like, will Squirreltown be somewhere you can actually go? Will some poor town be completely overrun with squirrels? Or is this part of dog mythology?" said Stewart.

"It is not a place with people," said Waldo. "It is only squirrels. I don't know where it is."

"We will be able to go there though," said Sassy.

"Oh yes, there will be many dogs going on vacations in Squirreltown," said Waldo.

"Wouldn't that be like taking your job on vacation with you?" said Stewart.

"I suppose," said Sassy. "But the truth is we like our job."

"Keeping the squirrels out is fun," said Waldo.

"We are vigilant," said Sassy.

"They are so afraid of us," said Waldo.

"And one day there will be no more squirrels," said Sassy.

"They will all be in Squirreltown," said Waldo.

"And then we can nap," said Sassy.

"So it doesn't bother you that your job is never done?" said Stewart.

"Well, we do it every day," said Waldo. "Like you, at school. You go to school every day, and now, at the end of the day, you can feel good about a good day's work, done. Or . . . hold on. Is this why you are always so worried? Because you do not feel like you have done a good day's work?"

"Maybe it's that, a little," said Stewart.

"Because you have done a good day's work!" said Sassy. "You are such a good human."

"We thought it was because school is a terrible place," said Waldo. "But now we have been there, and we know it is a great place, with delicious food and beautiful music."

"And running and catching," said Sassy.

"And recess," said Waldo. "Plus Ms. Twohey. She is probably the best teacher in the entire world."

"She's the only teacher you've ever known," said Stewart.

"That is not true," said Waldo. "We knew Dog Trainer Lady."

"Dog Trainer Lady was amazing. She was like a magician. She made treats appear from everywhere," said Sassy.

"See, even the dog trainer was better than Ms. Twohey," said Stewart.

"But she was a trainer," said Waldo. "And Ms. Twohey is a teacher. We learned to sit and stay from Dog Trainer Lady, but we learned multiplication from Ms. Twohey."

"What more could you want in a teacher?" said Sassy. "She's nice. She's smart. She's good at teaching things. My only complaint is that she doesn't reward us with **cookies** every time we get something right."

"She should do that," said Waldo. "Is that the problem, Stewart? Are you sad at school because she doesn't give you **cookies**?"

"That would help," said Stewart.

"Does she have a suggestion box?" said Waldo. "I'm totally going to suggest that to her."

"Good luck," said Stewart.

CHAPTER THIRTEEN

The next time he saw her, Waldo did tell Ms. Twohey that she should give the children **cookies** when they got something right.

"It would make them so happy," said Waldo. "US, I mean. All of us human children."

"We don't reward with food here," said Ms. Twohey. "I don't think children should get sweets for doing a good job. I think the reward is the knowledge gained."

"Sweets?"

"You said **cookies**."

"Oh, I meant something more like **beef cookies**."

"I have never heard of **beef cookies**, Salty."

"Well," said Waldo. "That is something we had all the time in Liver, Ohio. We got **beef cookies** to reward us for a job well done."

"Huh," said Ms. Twohey. "Well, time to hustle on into class. We have an exciting day of science experiments ahead of us."

Salty sat at their desk, and Ms. Twohey put a large box on a table at the front of the room.

"You all know what the five senses are," said Ms. Twohey. "Sight, touch, smell, hearing, and taste. Today we'll be working on some experiments to help you refine your knowledge of how each of those senses works for you in your day-to-day life."

"We already know all this stuff," said Bax. "We learned about the senses last year."

"That is because Bea Arthur Memorial Elementary School and Learning Commons is giving you a stellar education," said Ms. Twohey. "However, the state believes that you should be learning about the senses this year, and they're going to put it on the test. So we're doing a quick review of it today, just to make sure you all remember it. Plus we have some new students this year." She looked at Salty. Waldo smiled.

"This will just be an overview of the topic today," continued Ms. Twohey. "It'll be fun, and you might learn something new. But I know you can handle more. We'll get to more **meaty** topics later in the year."

"I am looking forward to that," said Waldo.

"Good," said Ms. Twohey.

"What kind of **meat**?" asked Waldo.

"I was talking about science, Salty," said Ms. Twohey.

"Do you think the **meat** topics will be tomorrow?" asked Waldo.

"No," said Ms. Twohey. She took five rubber balls out of the box and set them on the table in a line. Waldo's ears swiveled and he stared hard.

"Would someone pull the blinds down, please? Thank you. Now, what color are these balls?"

A girl named Arden raised her hand. "Orange, yellow, green, blue, and purple."

"Yellow, yellow, yellow, blue, and purple," Waldo said quietly.

"Very good," Ms. Twohey told Arden.

"Now I'll turn off the lights. What color are the balls?"

"They're grey," said Arden.

"You are a magic teacher!" said Waldo.

"That's because humans can't see colors in the dark," said Ms. Twohey.

"Moving on!" Ms. Twohey put three small black boxes on the table. Each had a round opening in the front covered by a piece of black fabric.

"I need a few volunteers to try to determine what the objects in these boxes are using only their sense of touch." Stewart raised his hand. Sassy nudged Waldo, and he raised his paw. The dogs loved volunteering for things and doing things with Stewart. Also they wanted Ms. Twohey to think they were good dogs.

"One more volunteer?" asked Ms. Twohey.

"Oh, what the hey," said Bax, raising his hand. "I'm bored anyway, might as well stand up for a while."

"Terrific," said Ms. Twohey. "We'll work down the line from left to right. You'll each stick your hand in and tell me what you think is in the box. And then I'll open it and we can all see if you were right. Go ahead, children!"

Stewart stuck his hand in the first box. "I don't know. It's . . . rough? Is it an old book?"

Bax stuck his hand in. "Nah, that's not a book. I think it's lizard skin."

Waldo sniffed the box. "It's sandpaper." He sniffed again. "Eighty-grit sandpaper."

"You didn't even put your hand in," said Bax.

"Sure I did. I was just really fast, like a superhero. You missed it."

Ms. Twohey opened the box and made a big show of pulling the item out. "Sandpaper! Salty is right! Do you see, though, how not being able to use all our senses can make it hard to understand what one of our senses is telling us? This isn't lizard skin at all, right, Bax? Okay, try the second box."

"It's scratchy and soft at the same time," said Stewart. "A sponge?"

"It feels like a teddy bear I had once," said Bax. "I mean, probably some dumb old bear."

Waldo made a big show of putting his paw into the box before leaning over to smell it. "It is a piece of fabric. Eighty percent acrylic, twenty percent wool. It is," he sniffed again, "plaid."

Ms. Twohey opened the box and lifted out a swatch of plaid fabric.

"How could you *feel* that it was plaid?" said Bax. "No one can feel that. You're cheating!"

"The way it is woven. I could feel that."

"Last box!" said Ms. Twohey.

"Ribbons," said Stewart.

"Dead worms, probably," said Bax.

"Grass," said Waldo. "Grass from behind the school. It was cut with a pair of scissors yesterday afternoon."

"Of course it's going to be right," said Bax.

And it was. Salty was very good at all the experiments Ms. Twohey had them do, but mostly because they could always smell what the answer was.

For the sound experiment, Ms. Twohey rang a gong. She played an accordion. She walked around the room, hitting a drumstick against various surfaces. And then she blew into a small metal tube.

"Hello!" said Waldo.

She blew into it again.

"Hi!" said Waldo. "what are you needing! We are here to help!"

The other students looked at Waldo quizzically.

"It's fine, Salty," said Ms. Twohey. "That's a dog whistle, students. We can't hear it, but dogs can, because their ears register higher frequencies than ours do." She blew into the whistle one more time.

"Yes, hi! Hello!" said Waldo.

"Moving on," said Ms. Twohey.

Salty was also the only one who got everything correct during the actual smell experiment, when they had to identify smells from scratch-and-sniff cards.

"**Nutmeg**," Waldo said, smelling the last card.

"You got all twenty-five," said Ms. Twohey. "That's astounding. You have one heck of a sniffer!"

"**I sure do**," said Waldo. "**I am a SuperSmeller. That's a thing. A lot of humans from Liver, Ohio, are also SuperSmellers.**"

"I bet you can smell how much learning is happening!" said Ms. Twohey. "I'm kidding, of course. But I bet you can. Right? You can smell what a good teacher I am?"

"**You are the best teacher. I can also tell that you had chicken curry for dinner last night and you had a fight with your boyfriend.**"

"He said it was too spicy! Oh, never mind. It's almost time to go home. Neaten your desks, everyone. Your only homework for tonight is to put the finishing touches on your big projects, since it's almost the very exciting day when you will be presenting them, as well as turning in the Information Sheet, without which, I will remind you, you have no hope and you will fail."

Stewart frowned as he put a book into his backpack. He looked into his desk to see if he should bring anything else. It was hard to tell. His desk was a mess of papers and pencils. He shoved the papers into the desk deeper, sighed, and zipped his backpack.

"Pretty cool how you can smell that stuff," said Bax.

"I am very cool," said Waldo.

"I didn't *say* you were cool," said Bax.

"Are you sure? It smelled like you did."

Bax tried to look angry but smiled despite himself, and went back to his desk.

"I've never seen Bax speechless before," said Stewart.

"He is our friend," said Waldo.

"I don't think so," said Stewart.

"I really hope we get to do **meat** science tomorrow," said Waldo.

CHAPTER FOURTEEN

That night, after dinner, Sassy was trying to nap, but something kept banging and waking her up.

"I think there's a squirrel in the house," she said. She tried to stand, but she was too groggy.

"If that's a squirrel, it's some kind of mega squirrel," said Waldo. "Or it's one squirrel that is extremely dense. That's a lot of banging. We need to investigate."

"Fine. Wait, I need to nap a little more. Stop looking at me like that. Fine, fine. Let's go."

The dogs crept up the stairs. Sassy was good at getting very low. She knew squirrels could not see her if she was very low.

"The banging is coming from Stewart's room!" said Waldo. "We have to save him from the giant or regular-size-but-oddly-heavy squirrel!"

"Maybe it's more than one squirrel."

"I hadn't considered that," said Waldo. "Do you think it might be?"

"I'm worried that they're coming into the house every day when we're at school," said Sassy.

"And you think maybe now they are staging their rebellion? Or do you think they've sent ahead one very large squirrel and one small, heavy squirrel to initiate the takeover? I bet these squirrels are very fierce, since they're the ones that were sent ahead as sentries."

"The only thing I'm sure about right now is that you're stalling. Let's just go in." Sassy scratched at the door and whined until Stewart opened it.

"Where are the squirrels?" asked Waldo, adopting what he assumed was a fighting stance. He looked around. He didn't see any squirrels. The room was a little messier than usual, but still, no squirrels.

"Squirrels? In here?" said Stewart.

"No squirrels?" said Sassy, tilting her head slightly.

"Of course there are no squirrels!" said Waldo. "We are so good at keeping all the squirrels out of the house! Why would there be any squirrels in here?"

"What was all that banging?" asked Sassy.

"Oh. I'm doing homework," said Stewart.

"What homework did Ms. Twohey give us where we get to bang around?" asked Waldo. "That sounds fun. I think I would have remembered that."

"I'm actually looking for my Information Sheet. I seem to have misplaced it."

"We can help you find it!" said Sassy. She was excited. Sassy liked being useful. "We'll be able to smell it."

"You will?"

"Sure," said Waldo. "Ms. Twohey gave it to you, right? If she touched it, it's going to have a very distinctive smell on it."

"What does Ms. Twohey smell like?" asked Stewart.

"Red pens, stickers shaped like stars, and antibacterial lotion," said Waldo.

"Big books, **turkey sandwiches**, and coffee," said Sassy.

"Breath mints," said Waldo.

"Rulers," said Sassy.

"**Chicken soup from a mix**," said Waldo.

"Novelty socks," said Sassy.

"Okay, fine," said Stewart. "If you can find the Information Sheet that would be amazing."

"You need that Information Sheet," said Waldo. "You will fail without it."

"I know! I know! You don't have to tell me!" said Stewart. "It's here somewhere."

"We can do this!" said Sassy. "Waldo and I will find it for you in one minute." The dogs sniffed around for one minute. They sniffed around for two minutes. Then ten. With every passing minute, Stewart looked more dejected.

"I'm going to fail," he said. "I need that Information Sheet. Where could it be?"

"We found lots of papers that Ms. Twohey touched," said Waldo, pawing at a stack of math worksheets and grammar lessons. "But none of them are the Information Sheet. Maybe we could make one. I bet Ms. Twohey wouldn't even be able to tell the difference."

Waldo found a crayon and started to make random purple streaks on a piece of paper. He closed one eye and looked at the paper. He smelled it. "Well, it smells good, at any rate. Maybe Ms. Twohey will be so distracted by how good crayons smell that she won't notice that this isn't an official Information Sheet. Sassy, what do you think? Sassy?" Sassy was napping on a pile of laundry on the floor. Waldo barked to wake her.

"What?" she said. "Did you find it?"

"No. We would have if you hadn't fallen asleep. I made this." He showed her his crayon markings.

"Good for you," said Sassy. "Is it a self-portrait?"

"No. It's an Information Sheet. Just fill this out and tape it to the big project that you have already completed and that is also somewhere in this room, although I do not see it."

"I'm doomed," said Stewart.

CHAPTER FIFTEEN

Stewart was even gloomier the next day. The dogs were in a great mood.

"Why are you so chipper?" asked Stewart on the walk to school.

"School is so fun! Everyone loves me," said Waldo.

"They love *us*," said Sassy. "I'm really the under-appreciated half of Salty."

"Plus I'm mostly sure there's no evil overlord, so that's a relief," said Waldo.

"Why are we still going to school?" said Sassy. "I forget. Shouldn't we be napping at home in the sun square?"

"We have to help Stewart with his big project!"

Stewart groaned.

"Plus also because now we love school," said Waldo.

It was true. Waldo loved school. He loved having humans make eye contact and smile at him. He loved singing and running and getting lunch. If the doom of the missing Information Sheet wasn't hanging over Stewart, it would really be the best.

In the middle of math, Waldo got a funny feeling.

"Sassy," he whispered, "I need to go out."

"Now that you bring it up, I do too," she whispered back.

"Stewart," said Waldo. "Where's the doggy door?"

"They're all regular doors," said Stewart. "There's no doggy door."

"Oh no," said Waldo. "That is bad. You hold it all day?"

"Oh!" said Stewart. "You need the bathroom."

"I do not want a bath."

"No, that's where we, you know, go to the bathroom," said Stewart.

"I don't want a bath either," said Sassy.

"I mean, it's where the toilets are," said Stewart. "Go tell Ms. Twohey you have to go the bathroom, and she'll give you a hall pass."

"MS. Twohey, I have to go to the bathroom," said Waldo.

"Sure, Salty," said Ms. Twohey. "As long as you really are going to the bathroom and not going into the hall to send covert messages to your operatives from Don Knotts Academy, telling them about my teaching methods."

"It is only the bathroom part," said Waldo. "Although you are a very good teacher."

Waldo and Sassy got a hall pass and went to find the bathroom.

"Am I looking at this right?" said Waldo. "There are two bathrooms. Which one are we supposed to use?"

"There are two bathrooms at home," said Sassy.

"But not right next to each other," said Waldo. "Maybe one of these isn't a bathroom at all. Maybe it's a secret **sandwich** room, and if you know the password, you get a **sandwich**."

"Is your nose broken?" said Sassy. "Because there's no **sandwich** anywhere near here."

Just then a boy walked out of one of the bathrooms.

"**Is there anyone else in there?**" Waldo asked the boy.

"Not that I know of," said the boy.

"Let's go in this one," said Sassy, "because it's empty."

"Wow! This sure is a cornucopia of smells," said Waldo as they walked in. "Let's just do our business and get out of here. Wait. What is this place? Why are there so many human toilets? And what are those weird sinks on the wall?"

Sassy nosed her snout into one of the stalls. "We didn't think this through at all. How are we going to pee in here?"

"Maybe there's a small tree somewhere," said Waldo. "Or a patch of grass."

"They don't have room for a small tree because there are so many toilets," said Sassy.

The dogs continued to look around, anxious, wondering what to do. Waldo sniffed at the garbage can. Sassy wandered into one of the stalls.

"Sassy, what's going on in there?" said Waldo. "Are you just staring at the human toilet?"

"I'm thirsty."

"Sassy, no! That is not allowed at Bea Arthur Memorial Elementary School!"

"Wait. Listen!" Sassy cocked her head to the side, moving her ear for maximum sonic reception. "Ms. Twohey's class is walking down the hall."

"It is recess time! I can smell it!" said Waldo.

The dogs quickly reassembled as Salty and raced out to the end of the line. As soon as the class got outside, they ran to a bush on the far side of the playground and did what they had to do.

"I feel one thousand times better," said Waldo. "Let's play tag or chase or fetch."

"You know we have more important work to do," said Sassy.

"We do?"

"Look over there."

"A squirrel!"

"Let's go," said Sassy. "We can do this."

"We're profession-als," said Waldo.

Sassy ran toward the squirrel. Waldo leaned in, making their team more aerodynamic, like professionals do. The squirrel ran up a tree.

"Do you see any more squir-rels?" said Sassy.

"I do not," said Waldo. "I assume any others ran off in terror when they saw us. We should wait here by this

tree in case this squirrel decides to fall off the branch and into my mouth."

"We could bring it home for dinner," said Sassy.

"Everyone would love that. When was the last time they ate squirrel for dinner?"

"I think it was never."

"They are missing out." said Waldo.

"Look! I found a **cheese cracker**!" said Sassy.

"What?"

"Someone must have dropped a snack. That **cracker** was great. It was shaped like a **tuna**. Do you think **tunas** are **cheese** flavored? I'm starving. Let's find another."

"It seems like maybe you're getting distracted."

"No, I'm not," said Sassy. "It's just . . . never mind."

"What is it?" said Waldo.

"I like our life. I like our schedule. I like waking up and checking for squirrels and going out the doggy door. I like getting breakfast and then napping in the sun square. I like Waggy Greeting Stewart when he comes in. I like that there's a basket of toys in the corner of the living room, and every day I can play with the toys, and then the next morning the toys are back in the basket. I haven't played with those toys in days. Plus the more dire fact that we've been coming to school every day and the squirrels notice. They know things. What if they've taken over the house? What if, every day, they come in and rub their squirrel fur all over the furniture? Then next week they'll be eating our food, and two weeks from now we'll be kicked out to the backyard and the squirrels will be sleeping in my bed. Remember last night? When we thought the squirrels were invading? That's going to happen any day now."

"Do you think that might really happen?"

"I don't know. Probably."

"Look at Stewart though."

Stewart sat on a swing, chewing on his thumbnail, staring at the wood chips on the ground. The dogs instinctively ran over to him. Stewart smiled and pet Waldo while Sassy leaned against his leg.

"Stewart?" asked Waldo.

"Yes?"

"You haven't done anything on the big project, have you?"

Stewart exhaled noisily. "Not really," he said. "No."

"We will help you!" said Sassy. "We can do this!"

"I haven't even picked a topic yet."

"That is not a problem," said Waldo. "We will help you pick a topic!"

"That might be a little bit of a problem," said Sassy. "But it will be okay. We know so much about so many topics, I think the hard part will really be choosing which one to do."

"Recess is over," said Stewart.

"As soon as we get home and nap and eat dinner and nap again, we will work on your project," said Sassy.

CHAPTER SIXTEEN

Ms. Twohey stood at the front of the class, beaming. "Students, I am so looking forward to tomorrow! The big day, when you all bring in your marvelous, thorough, and well-researched projects, along with, of course, your Information Sheets. I cannot wait to see all that you have put together!"

"I created a hybrid wheat plant that can sustain severe drought and flooding," said a girl.

"I discovered a new species of butterfly," said a boy.

"I built an isotope," said a girl.

"Me too!" said another boy.

"My project is so great," said Bax. "It's better than all of yours. What'd you do, Stewart? Whatever you did, it's not as cool as mine."

"It's a secret," said Stewart. "I want everyone to be surprised."

"Whatever," said Bax. "Mine's still better."

That night after dinner, Stewart paced in his room. Waldo paced too, while Sassy sat on the bed, trying to stay awake.

"So all you need to do is discover wheat or create your own form of government or build something impossible," said Waldo.

"That's too much," said Sassy. "We need to figure out what you already have, and just make that your project." She looked around. "Like, your project could be not putting away your laundry. Or being the best at giving belly rubs."

"I wish we could do a project," said Waldo.

"What would yours be about?" asked Stewart.

"I don't know. Squirrels, probably."

"Squirrels would be a fun project," Sassy agreed.

"The hard part would be narrowing it down," said Waldo. "I could do fifty different squirrel projects."

"I'd like to do a project about how we keep all the squirrels out of the yard," said Sassy.

"And out of the house!" said Waldo. "As soon as a squirrel even thinks about us, it runs right up a tree."

"Yeah it does," said Sassy. "We're so fierce."

"I wonder how it runs straight up a tree like that," said Stewart.

"Claws," said Waldo.

"And fully articulated ankle joints," said Sassy.

"Really?" said Stewart.

"Of course," said Sassy. "We're squirrel experts. We keep telling you that."

"Squirrels are mammals," said Waldo.

"They are omnivores," said Sassy. "That means they eat everything."

"Squirrels use their tails to help them balance," said Waldo.

"They also use their tails as umbrellas and blankets," said Sassy.

"And most of all they are terribly frightened of us," said Waldo.

"Also," said Sassy, "one day all the squirrels will pack their bags and move to Squirreltown."

"The squirrels will all form their own government and elect a council of squirrel elders," said Waldo.

"Okay, I think you're including some unsubstantiated dog lore now," said Stewart.

"Oh, it's all true," said Waldo.

"This is great," said Stewart. "I don't have the Information Sheet, but I can talk about all these facts, up until the Squirreltown part. I need a visual aid though. I wish I had a fake squirrel and tree or something."

"I have a squirrel!" said Sassy. "I'll be right back!" She ran out of Stewart's room, and returned a minute later holding a dog toy shaped like a squirrel.

"You've chewed on this a bit," said Stewart. "Didn't it have stuffing in it once?"

"It's still squirrel-shaped," said Sassy. "You can pretend to make it climb up the classroom walls."

"Son?" Stewart's dad knocked on the doorframe. "Your mother and I bought you this artisanal tree stump bedside table. The lady at the shop assured us that all the kids today love stump tables. She said something about how the youths enjoy a rustic sensibility. We got you the one with the bark still attached, because it matches your bedspread. Here you go!" He put a large tree stump inside the room, and scurried away.

"Thanks, Dad!" Stewart yelled down the hall. He turned to the dogs. "Well, that was convenient. I'd better get to work. I'm going to start writing down squirrel facts. I've got a lot of work to do before tomorrow!"

CHAPTER SEVENTEEN

The dogs and Stewart stumbled sleepily to Bea Arthur Memorial the next morning.

"I know I always say this," said Sassy, "but I could really use a nap."

"I feel okay," said Stewart, shouldering a gigantic tote bag with his project inside. "Yesterday I didn't have a project, and now I have this tote bag with a tree stump in it."

"I never knew that school would be all about tree stumps," said Waldo.

"I don't think it is," said Sassy. "All I know is that I need a nap."

The classroom was buzzing with excited students, ready to show off their projects. There was a robot, a volcano, and a lightning machine. There was a hand-made working cuckoo clock, a particle accelerator, and what appeared to be someone's baby brother. And every single one of them, except for Stewart's stump, had a properly-filled-out Information Sheet taped to it. Even the baby brother had one, though it had a lot of drool on it.

"Hey, Stew, whatcha got there, a log?" asked Bax. "My project is so much better than yours. Where's your info sheet?"

"It's here somewhere," said Stewart. "Let me know if you see it. Seriously. Where is it?"

Bax looked at Stewart's stump, then at Stewart. Stewart was mindlessly lifting up pencils and notebooks from his desktop, like he was looking for the Information Sheet.

"Where'd you have it last?" asked Bax.

"Yeah," said Stewart. "Oh, what? I don't know."

"You need to find it," said Bax. "A lot."

"Hello to my good friend, Bax," said Waldo. "I am looking forward to learning all about your project."

"Yeah, you are," said Bax.

"I hope it is about **hot dogs**, and then after we get free samples."

"Uh, yeah, that's pretty far off base," said Bax. "Is yours about **hot dogs**?"

"I wish. I became a student too late to do a project."

"Do you see Stewart's Information Sheet any-where?" said Bax. "It's totally gone."

"Maybe that human puppy ate it," said Waldo.

"Ah GAH!" said the baby.

"Don't blame the baby," said Bax.

"You humans have such interesting idioms," said Waldo.

"What do you mean, 'you humans'?" asked Bax.

"Oh, that's just a thing we say in Liver, Ohio," said Waldo.

Ms. Twohey clapped her hands to get everyone's attention. "We have a lot to do today. We need to get through everyone's presentations. Let's get started. When it's your turn, come up to the front of the room and hand me your Information Sheet. You'll have ten minutes to present your project."

And so began a long (though also fairly interesting) day of the dogs watching while Stewart worried about when he'd be called on, and how he'd explain his missing Information Sheet. They watched his classmates demonstrate the frog life cycle, the caterpillar life cycle, and the woolly mammoth life cycle. (They were fairly sure that woolly mammoths did not emerge from cocoons, but it was an interesting presentation regardless.) The minutes and presentations ticked on, and Stewart managed to hide behind his tree stump and avoid being called on.

"Okay!" said Ms. Twohey. "Today has been so educational! Except for the facts that some of you invented. But really mostly very educational. Two more to go! Bax? Stewart? Who wants to be next?"

Stewart made an involuntary whimpering noise.

"It's my turn now," said Bax authoritatively. "Today. I'd like to talk to you. About velocity. What is velocity? What is space? What is time? What is acceleration?"

Bax spent the next thirty minutes discussing the finer points of the physics of velocity, stopping often to pause dramatically. Everyone was mesmerized, mainly because they'd never heard Bax talk for so long without making a joke. The dogs were mesmerized because his presentation centered around discussing the velocity of balls, and Bax threw a ball from one end of the room to the other no less than seventy times while he spoke. Bax kept looking at the clock, and kept talking. Ms. Twohey tried to stop him several times, but Bax told her he had more to say, and he wasn't going to stop until he was done.

"And that," said Bax finally. "Is all I know. About. Velocity. And balls! And how velocity relates to time. And distance. And—" The bell rang. Bax bowed. The class applauded.

"Stewart, we'll have to do your project presentation tomorrow," said Ms. Twohey. "I'm so sorry we weren't able to get to you today."

"It's okay," said Stewart.

"I will catch up with you in a little while," said Waldo as Stewart was walking out of the room. "I have to talk to Ms. Twohey now."

Stewart looked suspicious but couldn't say anything, since Ms. Twohey was there, staring at them.

"It is okay," said Waldo. "I will see you at your home. Later."

"What did you want to discuss?" asked Ms. Twohey. "Do you want to discuss how other schools are trying to spy on me?"

"No, thank you," said Waldo. "I would like to discuss Information Sheets. I would like to have one. I know I did not have time to complete a project. But today was educational. And inspiring. And Information Sheets look like so much fun. Remember when you said you wish I could fill one out? I wish that too. Can I have one? To fill out? Or two, even? I love to fill out important forms for school."

"Really? Well, how can I turn that down? I love it when students want to do more work. Here you go." Ms. Twohey opened a drawer in her desk and handed Salty two Information Sheets.

"Thank you," said Waldo. "You are the very best teacher and I am learning so much."

"Oh, you," said Ms. Twohey.

CHAPTER EIGHTEEN

"We have saved the day!" said Waldo as he and Sassy burst into Stewart's room. "We are the winners! We are all good dogs!"

Waldo handed Stewart the Information Sheets. Sassy flopped on the rug and fell asleep immediately.

"Wait. Where did you find these?" said Stewart.

"Ms. Twohey gave them to us. She is the nicest."

Stewart sharpened his pencil. "After all this fuss, I'm going to use my neatest handwriting to fill this thing out." He took his time, writing carefully. After a while, he stopped writing and frowned.

"What is the matter?" said Waldo. "Is filling out the Information Sheet not as fun as we thought it would be?"

"It's just a little more involved than I expected. 'What are the educational benchmarks addressed by your project? How will your presentation help your classmates become functional adults? On a scale of one to ten, how amazing a teacher is Ms. Twohey?'"

"Twelve!" said Waldo. "She is twelve amazing!"

"Squirrels are so educational," said Sassy, yawning. "And they will help your classmates become functionable adults."

"How?" said Stewart. "After seeing everyone's projects today, it feels like my project might need a little bit more."

"Like maybe you should talk about how squirrels build a cocoon and after three years they crack it open and it's all acorns inside?" said Waldo.

"That's not true at all," said Stewart.

"It sounds true to me," said Waldo.

"The point is, squirrels can't be trusted," said Sassy.

"You know what we're all experts in now? Velocity. You should do something about the velocity of squirrels," said Waldo.

"What, like throw a squirrel to show how far it goes?" said Stewart.

"Yes!" said both dogs at once.

"You should definitely throw a squirrel," said Sassy.

"This is going to be the greatest day of my life," said Waldo. "Stewart throwing a squirrel is something I never realized I needed until right this moment."

"I guess I could throw the squirrel-shaped dog toy," said Stewart. "Though I'm not sure how throwing a squirrel will be educational."

"It will be *so* educational," said Sassy.

"It will teach everyone how unpredictable squirrels are," said Waldo. "You never know what's next with squirrels!"

"Squirrels are chaos!" said Sassy. "Also I think it will work best if you throw a real, live squirrel."

"First of all, no," said Stewart. "Second of all, even if I was going to do that, how would I get a squirrel? You two have been trying to catch a squirrel as long as I've known you, and you've never gotten close."

"Now, hold on a minute," said Waldo. "We are not trying to catch one."

"Oh, really?" said Stewart.

"We are trying to clear the area," said Waldo. "And we are doing such a good job."

"There are no squirrels in your room at all," said Sassy. "That proves what a good job we're doing. If we wanted to catch a squirrel, we could do it." She stood up suddenly, excited. "Do you? Do you want us to catch one? We'll go get one right now! Then you just have to hold on to it until tomorrow!"

"No, it's fine," said Stewart. "I don't need a squirrel. Let me finish filling out the Information Sheet."

The dogs stared at Stewart while he did his best to answer the questions about the educational quality of a project he'd just come up with the day before. They knew they were helping. It was always helpful to stare at humans doing a difficult task. Stewart wrote. He sighed. He stared at the ceiling. He wrote some more. He looked at the dogs, then wrote some more.

"There's something bugging me," said Stewart.

"Squirrels," said Waldo. "Squirrels are bugging you. They do that."

"No, it's not that. It's that I'm filling this out after everyone else already did their project."

"That's not your fault!" said Sassy. "You didn't have the Information Sheet until today!"

"Well, that actually is my fault. I lost it. And now I'm filling this out because you got me a new one."

"That's because we're the most helpful dogs ever!" said Waldo. "And total professionals."

"Right, but I think you've given me what is known as an unfair advantage. And if I add more to my project, if I make it about a squirrel's velocity, or purposely change everything to make it more like all the best presentations today, then that's cheating. I have to stick with what I would have presented today. We were lucky that I was last, and that Bax had so much to say."

"Bax really did have a lot to say!" said Waldo.

"He did!" Sassy agreed. "He talked for three times as long as anyone else, plus his presentation involved a lot of balls."

"So many balls," said Waldo.

"There were balls in that science project about colors too," said Sassy.

"Why didn't you tell us that there were so many balls in school?" said Waldo.

"I didn't want to make you feel bad about having to stay home, I guess," said Stewart.

"If you cannot add more to your project, does that mean you will not fill out the Information Sheet either?" said Sassy. "You didn't have that this morning."

"Oh, I'm totally filling this out. Filling this out isn't cheating, since I had an Information Sheet once. But I'm going to stick with my presentation about squirrel facts. It will still be educational."

"So educational!" agreed Sassy. "It's important everyone knows the truth about squirrels."

"Make sure you talk about Squirreltown," said Waldo. "And tell them how the squirrels are plotting an overthrow of the humans. Tell them not to leave acorns or **walnuts** outside. Or **tiny peanut butter sandwiches**. I don't know if anyone leaves trays of **tiny sandwiches** outside, but if they did, it would definitely help the squirrels."

"Do humans do that?" said Sassy. "Humans should not do that. They should also not build tiny cozy squirrel huts high in the trees, with tiny blankets and hand-knit squirrel hats." She yawned.

"I don't know where you two are getting your information," said Stewart. "But all of that is wrong. I think. I'm pretty sure."

"You can never be completely sure," said Waldo. "The squirrels control everything. Before you know it, you'll be making them **sandwiches** and sewing them mittens."

"Remember this," said Sassy. "Squirrels mean chaos."

"They are watching our every move," said Waldo.

"I'll be right back," said Stewart. He left the room and came back a few minutes later with new rawhide bones. "Chew on these for a while. And forget about squirrels. You are thinking way, way, way too much about squirrels."

"Who said anything about squirrels?" said Waldo.

"Hand over the bones now," said Sassy, "please."

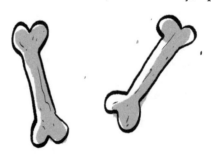

CHAPTER NINETEEN

The dogs managed not to worry much about squirrels the next morning either. There weren't any squirrels in the backyard, no stealthy, crafty humans had left out tiny seed cakes or squirrel scarves, and Stewart was so happy and relaxed he hummed a tune on the way to school.

"It is a good thing we came to school and enrolled as a human," said Waldo.

"I like the part about how we get a pile of **meat** for lunch every day," said Sassy. "We never used to get lunch before. Why didn't we get lunch? The humans eat every nine minutes. And we only get breakfast and dinner."

"Sometimes you get **cookies**," said Stewart. "For snacks."

"**Snack cookies** are good," said Waldo.

"**Meat cookies** are even better," said Sassy.

"Let's not complain right now," said Waldo. "Everything is going pretty well. We saved Stewart from the evil overlord—"

"What evil overlord exactly?" said Stewart.

"The Information Sheet," said Waldo.

"Oh yeah," said Stewart. "That evil overlord."

"And now our boy is humming and will do a very important and educational lecture about squirrels today to his classmates. And I bet he's going to impress Ms. Twohey."

"Do you think if he impresses her, she'll give us a **cookie**?" said Sassy.

"I sure hope so," said Waldo.

Salty sat at their desk while Stewart made sure he had everything ready for his presentation.

"Did you bring fireworks?" Waldo whispered to Sassy.

"I don't think so, but this trench coat has a lot of pockets. Why?"

"I just want Stewart's presentation to be spectacular," said Waldo. "So many of the presentations were spectacular."

"Some of them were ludicrous," said Sassy. "Two were boring. Some were entertaining. One had an eruption."

"The volcano didn't erupt like it was supposed to."

"I was talking about the baby."

"Oh, right. Anyway, I think fireworks would be spectacular."

"We'll have to rely on Stewart to make the presentation spectacular all on his own."

"I guess."

But the dogs had to wait. Ms. Twohey made everyone do math work, reading work, and spelling work before it was time for Stewart to give his presentation.

"Stewart is smelling more nervous with every passing minute," said Waldo.

"I know," said Sassy. "This is like sitting next to a chihuahua."

"Not all chihuahuas are nervous," said Waldo. "Remember Buster?"

"Was that the tiny dog who used to punch me in the face?"

"Yes."

"That dog was feisty."

"Yes."

"Do you think Stewart is feisty?"

"Maybe."

"Now you smell nervous."

"I want Stewart to win."

"Is it a competition? Will there be a winner?"

"Isn't there always?"

Ms. Twohey clapped her hands. "Finish up your spelling dioramas and let's get ready to hear our last presentation. Boy, all those hot glue guns you're using sure made it warm in here. I'm going to open a window." She slid three of the classroom's windows open and then nodded at Stewart. "Whenever you're ready, go ahead."

Stewart brought the Information Sheet to Ms. Twohey and handed it to her. He carried his log to the front of the room. He kept the squirrel dog toy in his tote bag. He was going to bring it out at just the right moment. He wanted to create some suspense.

Meanwhile, Waldo sensed a movement out the window, and smelled a telltale scent wafting through the screen. Sassy sensed it too, her body tense, a low growl starting in her throat. Waldo stomped on her head to get her to shut up.

"Hey," she said. "Ow."

"Everything okay, Salty?" said Ms. Twohey.

"My stomach is grumbling. I think I need my daily midday **meat** pile. Or. Yes! I need to go out the doggy door!"

"Pardon?" said Ms. Twohey.

"The bath place, I mean," said Waldo. "I need to go to the room of bathing but where you can't actually take a bath."

"The bathroom?"

"I just said that."

"Are you sure?"

"I am very sure."

Ms. Twohey gave Salty the hall pass and the dogs ran out of the room, past the bathroom, and out the door. They instinctively broke apart out of the trench coat. They ran fast and low, knowing they'd cover more ground as two dogs, until they made it to the base of a big oak tree, circling.

"There he is!" said Waldo.

"I see him, I see him!" said Sassy.

This squirrel was so totally getting sent to Squirreltown.

"Are you ready?" said Waldo.

"I've never been more ready," said Sassy. "Let's do this. This squirrel is going down."

The squirrel was, in fact, going up. Farther up the tree. The dogs circled at the base of the trunk, growling, until Waldo said, "NOW!" and then they began to bark. The squirrel fluffed his tail at them.

"I'm going to jump on your shoulders. Then we'll be taller and we can reach him."

Waldo climbed onto Sassy, which did make him taller, but he was still about fifteen feet shorter than the squirrel. Waldo stretched as high as he could.

"Almost," he said, reaching, gritting his teeth. "I've almost got him."

Sassy looked up. "I don't think you're using the word 'almost' correctly."

Waldo shifted. "Hey, Stewart is giving his presentation. We're missing it."

"But. This squirrel."

"I know. I don't know what to do."

"What's Stewart saying?"

"Shh. Something about squirrels being able to climb up and down trees because of their toes."

"What else?"

"I think he's showing them how the bark on a tree is easy for squirrel toes to grip."

"Should we go back in?"

"Let's bark some more, and then go back in."

So they went back to barking, and the squirrel continued his nonchalant and sinister tail fluffing. The squirrel tauntingly climbed a few feet back down the tree, getting closer, which made the dogs bark even more.

"Just a minute," they heard Ms. Twohey say. "I'm going to close these windows so those darn dogs aren't so disruptive."

The squirrel said, "Ch ch ch ch ch."

Ms. Twohey closed one window.

The squirrel fluffed his tail and ran up the tree and out on a branch.

Ms. Twohey closed another window. The dogs started jumping as far as they could up the tree.

The squirrel gave one last flourishing fluff, ran down the branch, and leapt, flying through the air, landing on the ledge of the last open window. The squirrel used his amazing grippy toes and claws to dislodge the screen and jump into the classroom.

"Holy cats," said Waldo. "Did that just happen?"

"We've got to get back in there! Come on."

They quickly reassembled themselves in the trench coat, and then realized they were locked out of the school, and had to go around to the front door to get buzzed in.

"Hello?" said Dottie.

"Doodie. Hello. It is Salty. From Liver, Ohio. We are locked out of this fine school."

The door opened. "What are you doing out here?" said Dottie. "You shouldn't be outside by yourself. Were you running away?"

"I was not running away, I was running toward. Thank you for letting me inside. I have to go. I have learning to do."

"You need to fill out this Unauthorized Outside Access form," said Dottie.

"You sure do love your forms here!"

"What?"

"There were not as many forms to fill out in Liver, Ohio."

"I'll get you a clipboard."

"But it's not my birthday."

"What?"

"And if it was, I would want a **meatball**, not a clipboard."

"But."

"Goodbye! I have learning to do!" Sassy ran down the hall before Dottie could do anything.

160

CHAPTER TWENTY

The classroom was in complete chaos. Desks were overturned. A spelling diorama was hanging from the ceiling. The students were running in all directions, screaming, and the squirrel was chattering and leaping from bookshelf to bookshelf. Ms. Twohey had a broom and was chasing the squirrel, yelling, "Shoo! Shoo!"

Stewart stood at the front of the room, one hand on his tree stump, one hand on his forehead.

"There you are!" he said. "Where have you been? I was just describing how far squirrels can jump and this actual real, live squirrel started jumping all over the class."

"What good news," said Waldo.

"How is that good news?"

"Now your presentation will be memorable. This is spectacular, huh?"

"He's right," whispered Sassy from beneath the trench coat. "You should keep going."

Stewart looked at his classmates, who were, at that moment, huddled in the corner opposite the squirrel. The squirrel was sitting casually on top of a globe. Ms. Twohey stood between the students and the squirrel with her broom, although it was becoming clear she wasn't sure how to sweep the squirrel out of the classroom.

"As you can see," said Stewart, his voice shaky, "squirrels use their tails for balance. By shifting his weight and counterbalancing with his tail, he's able to stand on that thin piece of metal on top of the globe."

The squirrel jumped from the globe to the top of Ms. Twohey's desk. Stewart screamed a little.

"Okay, great. Did you see how he spread his body wide while he was jumping?" Stewart pointed at the squirrel. "That's so he can control his speed and direction, like the sail on a ship."

Bax moved slowly from the corner, sliding into his chair.

"You can also see," said Stewart, "how strong and powerful his back legs are. He uses those to propel himself off of branches. That's how he's able to jump so far. See how small he is? He can jump so far that it's like if you could jump over a building."

A few more students very carefully made their way back to their desks.

The squirrel sniffed at Stewart's log stump.

"Let's see if we can convince him to climb up this simulated tree so he can show us how he uses his articulated ankle joints. Does anyone happen to have an acorn?"

"Sure, I do," said Bax, who dug an acorn out of his pocket and expertly tossed it to Stewart, who placed it on top of the stump. The squirrel lifted his nose a bit, sniffing.

"Oh, good," said Stewart. "Squirrels have highly developed senses of smell. It's how they find their food. They can smell if the food is rotten, so they won't even bother climbing the tree to get it. Or they can smell if it's a good acorn."

"My acorn's not rotten," said Bax.

"I know," said Stewart. "That was just part of my presentation. You can see that this acorn is very fresh"—Stewart looked pointedly at Bax—"and . . . there he goes, up the fake tree! Everyone, look at his feet, how he grips the bark!"

Most of the students were sitting in chairs or on the floor in front of Stewart, and they all said, "Ooooooh!" when they saw how well the squirrel could climb.

"Now, everyone watch, if we're lucky he'll . . . yes! Look at that! He can expand his cheeks to hold nuts and other food so he can carry it to other places. He probably has a store of food for the winter. He'll eat some now, and save some for the cold months."

Salty was still standing off to the side of Ms. Twohey's desk, proudly watching Stewart, and also not wanting to move, since the squirrel would surely smell the dogs. Waldo watched the squirrel, who was shaking his tail a bit more aggressively, rotating his tiny ears, and sniffing the air. "He is wanting to leave now," Waldo whispered to Stewart. Stewart nodded.

"Everyone," said Stewart, improvising. "It's time to help this squirrel get back outside. I want you to stand up very carefully and form two lines between this desk and that open window. We're going to create a tunnel so he knows how to get out. In squirrel lingo, they call that a 'magic bridge.'" Waldo cocked his head at Stewart, who shrugged. The students stood in two rows. The squirrel was standing on the log stump now, but was moving more nervously.

"Don't forget to tell them about Squirreltown," whispered Waldo.

"Okay, now everyone, hold real still, and don't say anything." Stewart picked up the log stump with the squirrel on top of it, and started to walk. "I am entering the magic bridge." The squirrel shifted and made a loud chattering noise.

"This is not going to work," Sassy whispered to Waldo.

"The magic bridge always works," he whispered back.

"The magic bridge is something Stewart just made up thirty seconds ago." Sassy watched Stewart walking slowly with the log. One of the students moved back slightly to let Stewart by, and in that moment, a beam of sunlight came through the window. "Oh. Oh no."

"Sassy, what? Oh no. Don't."

ACHOO ACHOO ACHOO ACHOO ACHOO ACHOO ACHOO ACHOO ACHOO ACHOO ACHOO ACHOO ACHOO ACHOO

But she did. Sassy sneezed. Waldo hunched over and pretended it was his own sneeze. The thing with Sassy sneezing was, she always did it fifteen times in a row. The other thing was, the squirrel knew the difference between a human sneeze and a dog sneeze, even if no one else in that classroom could tell. The squirrel froze for a second. Stewart moved forward, still carrying the log.

"YIPPEE!" the squirrel yelled, jumping up and bouncing off of Stewart's face and onto the other students' heads. Stewart had been partially right. The magic bridge was useful. But mostly so the squirrel could have a line of children's heads to leap across to get to the open window.

Once a squirrel starts leaping on heads, it's very hard to stand still and straight in a neat line. Everyone started screaming. The dogs could no longer control their dog instincts and started chasing the squirrel, mostly toward the open window, but also just chasing in general, so the squirrel did not go straight out the window as planned.

With every movement of the squirrel, the children screamed louder. Ms. Twohey still had the broom and was doing a complex martial arts routine, both to scare away the squirrel and to reassure the students.

Salty chased the squirrel to the books. Then they chased the squirrel to the computers. Waldo took the skeleton's leg bone in his mouth and growled menacingly. Waldo had hoped to threaten the squirrel with one bone, but they all stayed attached, so he did his best to shake the skeleton back and forth in a frightening manner. Finally they chased the squirrel from the maps to the math center to the writing corner and out the window, banging the skeleton's head three times on the windowsill in triumph as the squirrel hollered insults from the tree outside. Ms. Twohey slammed the window shut, and the students cheered.

"Well done, Salty," said Ms. Twohey.

"We know what we are doing," said Waldo. "We know all about Squirreltown."

"Now drop the fibula."

"I am telling the truth."

"No, the fibula. That's the name of that bone you're holding."

"You really are a great teacher."

"You'd better believe it. You definitely need to stop licking that bone though."

"I'm from Liver, Ohio."

"I know, Salty. I know."

Waldo dropped the skeleton, and Sassy sat down, wondering if there was any way she could take a nap.

CHAPTER TWENTY-ONE

The door to the classroom swung open, and Ms. Barkenfoff, the principal, burst in.

"Just what is going on in here?" she said. "I could hear screaming and banging. It sounds like some sort of rock-and-roll shenanigans."

"No shenanigans!" said Waldo. "Just learning. Ms. Twohey . . . you know Ms. Twohey? Our great teacher?" Ms. Twohey waved from near the windows, still catching her breath.

"MS. Twohey is the best teacher," Waldo went on. "She knows that the way students learn best is through hands-on learning. We were doing an oral report, and a big project, and a science experiment all rolled into one today. Plus there was math in there, I think. And gym. Definitely some gym mixed in. It was amazing and so incredibly educational."

Ms. Barkenfoff looked around the room. The children were smiling and nodding.

"I learn a ton every day," said Bax. "But I learned the most today."

"I think MS. Twohey probably read that article that came out recently in that educational teacher magazine that said that students learn best when they are occasionally allowed to scream and run around and bang on stuff and turn desks over," said Waldo.

Ms. Twohey was next to them now but was still speechless. She honestly wasn't even sure what had just happened.

"Oh yeah, I heard about that," said Stewart. "It's called primal teaching. Or paleo teaching. One of those."

"Good one," said Bax, and fist-bumped Stewart.

"Is that true, Ms. Twohey?" asked Ms. Barkenfoff.

"Mostly," said Ms. Twohey. "We were definitely learning. It was an extremely educational afternoon. You know what they say! You can't make a student smarter without breaking a few desks!"

"Do they say that?" asked Ms. Barkenfoff.

"They sure do," said Ms. Twohey.

"So everything is fine, then?" said Ms. Barkenfoff.

"You bet! Now, if you'll excuse us, we have some desks to put back together before the end of the day. Students! Let's start putting everything back where it belongs!"

Everyone started picking up the mess, still laughing and talking about how amazing Stewart's presentation had been.

"That was the most fun I've ever had in school," said Bax. "You should get that squirrel to come in every day."

"Thanks," said Stewart, "but you should thank Salty. I think Salty had more to do with training that squirrel."

"Don't thank me," said Waldo. "It was just a thing that happened. But it was definitely spectacular. And it proves the thing we always say in Liver, Ohio: Squirrels are chaos."

"And thanks for yesterday," said Stewart to Bax. "I know you were just doing your presentation, but it was really helpful to have you talk for so long. Because I left my Information Sheet at home."

"I know," said Bax. "I knew you didn't have it."

"You did?"

"Yeah, sure. I could, like, just tell. Figured I'd take up the rest of the day so you could find it."

"Well, it was really nice of you. You saved my hide. Thanks."

"No problem. The least I could do for my best friend."

"Your what?"

"You know."

"I don't think I do. I thought you hated me."

"Why would you think that?"

"Because you said you're a bully and you're always making fun of me."

"No, that's my last name. Thabully. Bax Thabully. And sorry about making fun of you. That's just how they do it where I'm from. We let people know we like them by making fun of them. I forget sometimes that some people think that's rude."

"Oh."

"See, I told you he smelled like a cocker spaniel," said Waldo.

"Cocker spaniel? Well, I don't know about that. I think of myself more as a Great Dane."

"Hmm," said Waldo.

"Hey, I think I got your desk by mistake, Stewart!" said Arden. "I was cleaning out the papers and I found this Information Sheet with your name on it, crumpled up in the back. Also this page from a notebook with doodles of dogs on it."

"What? No way!" said Stewart.

"What's this Information Sheet you gave me, if your Information Sheet is right there?" said Ms. Twohey.

"I. Uh."

"Look, MS. Twohey! I filled out an Information Sheet too!" said Waldo, pulling the piece of paper with random purple crayon marks on it out of one of the trench coat pockets.

"What is this?"

"Art?"

Ms. Barkenfoff was at the door again. "Ms. Twohey!" she shouted.

"Oh, you're back," said Ms. Twohey. "Interrupting our learning again."

"Great news!" said Ms. Barkenfoff. "The National Organization of Superior Education just dropped this off!" She held a framed certificate out to Ms. Twohey.

"The NOSE? What could they possibly have for me? Oh! Oh my goodness. Oh gracious. Oh, I have to sit down." Ms. Twohey sat in a chair and hugged the certificate.

"What is it, Ms. Twohey?" asked Waldo.

"It's the Good Teacher Award. I won! I'm the Good Teacher of the Year."

"You are a good teacher," said Waldo. "You are a good teacher every year."

"Do you think so?" said Ms. Twohey. "I wonder . . . well, you showed up right around the time they start evaluating for this award. I thought you were a spy from the Don Knotts Technology and Arts Learning Academy."

"I am not a spy."

"But maybe you were one of the NOSE evaluators."

"I am good at smelling."

"Are you?"

"Yes?"

"Huh."

"Right now you smell like the **cottage cheese** you had for breakfast. You put **sunflower seeds** in it today. You don't usually do that."

"So you are from NOSE?"

"I have a nose."

"A NOSE membership card, you mean?"

"Is that a thing humans have? Membership cards for every body part? I have never heard of that before."

The bell rang.

"Phew!" said Ms. Twohey. "What a day! Thanks for helping put the room back together, everyone. You're all amazing students. See you tomorrow! Oh, Stewart, come here for a moment."

Stewart nervously shouldered his backpack and went to Ms. Twohey's desk.

"Great job today," she said. "I just wanted to let you know that you're getting an A++ on the big project. I wasn't sure what you were going to do it on, since you hadn't said anything about it, but I'm very impressed."

"Really? Wow! Thanks!" said Stewart.

"So . . . he won? He won! You won!" said Waldo.

"Won what?" asked Ms. Twohey.

"Never mind, come on, let's go," said Stewart, and walked out of school with Salty.

"Today was a lot of fun," said Waldo.

"You know what? It was," said Stewart. "I never thought I'd say this, but I really like school now. Thanks to you guys. You're such good dogs."

"I really like school too," said Waldo.

"But maybe sometimes we will say we are on a research vacation or an undercover investigation or a secret field trip," said Sassy. "So we can stay home and nap."

"Hey, it's a really nice day," said Stewart, opening the back gate to let the dogs into the backyard. "Let's go run around in the park."

And so they did.

That night at dinner, the dogs ate their **kibble** and then half dozed on the kitchen floor, relaxed and happy, knowing they had saved Stewart from the evil overlord. Stewart told his parents most of the details about his squirrel project. Stewart's mom told a story about running out of printer toner.

And then Stewart's dad said, "You know what's the weirdest thing? I found this old trench coat that I used to wear in college. I haven't seen this thing in ages, but I just found it on the floor by the back door. I'm pretty sure I had it dry cleaned before I put it away in the closet, but it's covered in dirt and grass stains now."

Both dogs stood up. Stewart knew he should say something, but he wasn't sure what.

"I suppose I should just throw it away," said Stewart's dad.

"NO!" said Stewart, Waldo, and Sassy at once, though to Stewart's parents, it just sounded like the dogs were barking.

"I want it," said Stewart.

"Well okay, then," said Stewart's dad.

The dogs lay back down, and Stewart covered them with the trench coat, tucking them in like it was a blanket, and they both fell deep asleep, snoring.

 **Julie Falatko** writes quirky books about misunderstood characters trying to find their place in the world. She is the author of *Snappsy the Alligator (Did Not Ask to Be in This Book)*, which was published to four starred reviews and coverage in the New York Times and People Magazine. She is also the author of *Snappsy the Alligator and His Best Friend Forever (Probably)* as well as many more forthcoming books. To learn more about Julie, please visit juliefalatko.com.

 **Colin Jack** is the illustrator of a number of books for children including *If You Happen to Have a Dinosaur, Under the Bed Fred, 1 Zany Zoo* and the Galaxy Zack series. He also works as a story artist and character designer in the animation industry and has been involved in the production of *Hotel Transylvania, The Book of Life, The Boss Baby*, and *Captain Underpants: The First Epic Movie*. Born in Vancouver, Colin currently resides in California, with his wife and two sons.